to
SWAY
A
SOUL

MUNG BEAN PRESS

Hardcover Dust Jacket Design: saintjupit3rgr4phic
Case cover and paperback Design: Ireen Chau
Interior Illustrations: Ireen Chau
Editing: Snow Ridge Press
Book Design and Typesetting: Enchanted Ink Publishing

The text type was set in Garamond Premier Pro

ISBN: 978-1-962634-06-9 (Paperback)
ISBN: 978-1-962634-05-2 (Hardcover)

Thank you for your support of the author's rights.

https://ireenchau.wixsite.com/website

For the artists who have bargained their soul away

to capitalism—may you find joy in creating art again.

WRITTEN AND ILLUSTRATED
BY IREEN CHAU

PROLOGUE

O NCE UPON A TIME, THERE was a boy who was afraid.

It was an inconvenient thing, as he had a sister to protect, and they both lived on the streets of a great city where the people were selfish and corrupt and cruel.

Some days they starved. Other days, the boy stole stale buns from a street vendor.

Every day, he was terrified.

But for his sister's sake, he pretended not to be. Shivering in their meager shelter, he told her stories of brave warriors and noble heroes who rode upon great steeds and gave starving children a home in their massive mansions.

The sister listened with delight, truly believing that a faceless hero would someday make life better for them. The boy loved her, so he let her believe, even when he knew that the men who owned mansions were no heroes—and that they wanted their massive homes all to themselves.

One fortunate day, the boy acquired a job as an errand boy for an herbalist shop. He was able to buy fresh buns from the street vendor and new clothes for them both. He let his sister guard over their meager wealth in a little embroidered pouch.

This would be her responsibility, he told her, and she accepted it eagerly.

The sister looked up to him with awe and admiration. She had no need for heroes when she had her brother.

But there were others on the streets who envied what the siblings had. A group of boys, since hardened by the cruelty of the streets, decided to take it for themselves. They cornered the sister and demanded she hand over the pouch and all it held.

With bravery fit for the warriors in her brother's stories, the sister refused.

And she paid dearly for it.

The boy stood frozen as the cruel group descended. He was so afraid, even as he wished for the courage to save her.

Eventually, blow by blow, he no longer had a sister to save.

AT THE EDGES OF THE city lay a great bamboo forest. Some spots were so dense and shadowed that many believed they were breeding grounds for *yao guai*, sprites and demons that brought mischief and bad luck.

There was a demon. It was a mere bamboo sprite, hidden in the dense corner of a forest, but it had lofty goals. If it had a human soul, it would be able to cultivate into an immortal.

It was to this corner the boy ran to, overcome with grief.

Demons fed off sorrow and strife. A boy grieving was the perfect target. With cloying words and promises of comfort, the bamboo sprite persuaded him to relinquish his soul.

The boy agreed. He had nothing left to lose.

His soul was small and young, but it was a bright, strong one nonetheless—taking the shape of a dragon. Even removed, it clung to him in golden tendrils like fibers of a lotus root, stretching endlessly as he walked further and further from the forest.

In the demon's grasp, the dragon soul writhed and fought.

Souls always returned to their rightful bodies. It was the way of the universe for things to settle into their natural order. So, with magic dripping in darkness, the demon trapped the dragon in an enchanted scroll where it would be blind to the boy's whereabouts.

For now, the demon slept. It was a patient thing. After a hundred years, it would check on it again. By then, the soul's connection to the boy would be severed. Mortals never lived long.

As for the boy, he returned to the city, numb to everything. He would never be afraid now.

But neither would he ever love.

PART I

To Change a Fortune

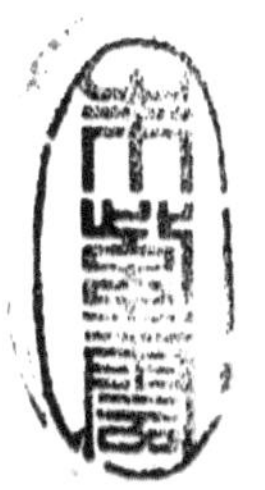

1

THE MAGISTRATE WAS SKINNIER THAN Zhi Lan expected.

Ma and Ba always said the rich had ten courses for every meal—it was a luxury only money could afford. Up until now, Zhi Lan had pictured everyone in the upper class to be plump and well-fed.

"Thank you all for coming to celebrate with me!" Magistrate Bu raised his wine cup with a scrawny hand to the guests scattered across his expansive courtyard.

In addition to his wiry frame, he had a thin mustache and a pasty complexion, exacerbated by his midnight blue robes. In short, he wasn't handsome at all. What a shame for Lady Bu, who sat beside him in elaborate robes, exuding beauty and elegance.

Zhi Lan shifted in her seat as her stomach growled. She had been far too nervous to eat that morning, and the sheer amount of food in her proximity seemed to taunt her. Before her was a perfect pyramid of colorful fruit and steaming pork buns dyed pink to resemble peaches. Porcelain dishes of savory meat, pickled vegetables, and white, pillowy rice peppered each low table where the banquet guests sat in the courtyard, shaded by the lilac wisteria trees swaying gently in the evening breeze.

Zhi Lan had never seen so much food or so much beauty at once. And to think *this* was the place she was to live...

"I feel it a duty of mine to bolster new talent in Zhu City," the magistrate said. Zhi Lan hadn't registered when he'd begun to speak. "I have recently taken under my patronage the up and coming scholar painter, Dan Li Chen. He is here this evening to present us with his most recent masterpiece."

The guests applauded, murmuring amongst themselves.

Master Dan sat serenely beside Zhi Lan, his snowy white scholar's robes the same shade as his trimmed beard and neat top knot. He was as old as Zhi Lan's grandfather, perhaps older, but he had recently made a name for himself as one of the greatest mountain and river painters across several counties. Zhi Lan had been under his tutelage for nearly a year and had grown quite fond of the old man. She couldn't have been more proud of him—and herself. After all, his wins were her wins.

Ma always said that a young woman was never taken seriously. The more time Zhi Lan spent in the city, the more she realized that was true. Without Master Dan, her passion for painting was a mere feminine hobby, not a serious pursuit. She only had respectability as Master Dan's student. For the time being, she cherished this. One day, when her master reached the heights of fame, she'd be able to pursue her own path and make a name for herself with his illustrious recommendation.

"Ready, Zhi Lan?" Master Dan asked in a low voice.

Zhi Lan clutched the heavy silk scroll in her hands and nodded. The evening was warm as it was late spring easing into early summer. Beads of sweat coated the back of her neck, though she couldn't entirely blame it on the balmy weather.

Together, they stood and made their way to the center of the courtyard. Master Dan clasped his hands before him and bowed low to the magistrate. Zhi Lan followed suit, holding the scroll out before her with both hands. Her arms trembled. This was the start of something monumental—the first step on the path of being a self-sustaining painter like her master. She hoped her parents would be proud.

"It is my honor to unveil my newest painting for your guests, my lord," Master Dan said.

Magistrate Bu waved a hand. "Yes, yes! Do not keep us in suspense. Bring it up."

Zhi Lan stepped forward, keeping her head lowered, and let the magistrate's young steward take the painting from her hands.

Magistrate Bu of Zhu City was known to be a great collector of art. Every few years, he would take a new artist under his wing and commission a piece for his private collection.

Zhi Lan was thrilled Master Dan had been singled out this year. She hoped they'd be allowed to see the magistrate's famous collection. If the art was anything like Master Dan's work, his lordship had good taste.

"They say Zhu City has known no other painter so accomplished," Lady Bu said, her voice soft and melodious. "I look forward to seeing your work."

"You flatter this humble servant, your ladyship," Master Dan said. "I cannot take all the credit—my student has been of great help to me."

Zhi Lan bowed even lower, blushing. But the stone-paved ground did not keep her interest for long, and she couldn't help but peek up at the dais. She was surprised to find Magistrate Bu staring at her.

Zhi Lan flicked her gaze to the ground again and shuffled backwards until she was safely behind Master Dan.

The steward unrolled the scroll, revealing the masterpiece she and Master Dan had painstakingly worked on for the past three months—and the sole reason why they were here now. This was the painting that caught Magistrate Bu's eye when Master Dan had first showed it off at a local tea house.

He had painted it on site on Shui Jin Mountain, where the waterfalls had sparkled like quartz under the sun and the rocks had burst with flora and fauna. The scene depicted the great waterfall, framed by a foreground of bamboo and a background of misty mountains, washed with a greenish blue haze, evoking a sense of serene mystery.

Master Dan's style was fine-lined and meticulous. Though each subject was carefully rendered, he occasionally let his brushstrokes bloom and bleed, bringing life and expression to an otherwise tight painting. Zhi Lan had prepared all the necessary pigments, and even helped Master Dan with the foliage in the foreground. She knew every line and mark that made this masterpiece. She couldn't wait to apply that knowledge to her own work one day.

The courtyard exploded into a smattering of applause and exclamations.

"An excellent painting!"

"Magistrate Bu has impeccable taste."

"His lordship certainly has an eye for talent!"

Master Dan turned to her, eyes glimmering, and whispered, "It appears they like it."

Zhi Lan beamed.

The banquet went on, and the guests, including her and Master Dan, were encouraged to eat and drink their fill. She couldn't believe this was going to be her new life. Traveling with Master Dan to paint stunning locales had been far more exciting than her days on the farm, but this! Sitting with officials and scholars, speaking with them and feasting with them, was beyond anything Zhi Lan had ever imagined.

She spent the evening in awed silence, content to just eat and observe.

When dusk came and the skies grew dim and hazy, Magistrate Bu approached their table. After exchanging pleasantries and toasting Master Dan with a cup of wine, he said, "Come, Li Chen. Let me give you a tour of the grounds. And afterward, I have treasures to show you."

Master Dan and Zhi Lan were led across the main courtyard to the private courtyard behind the central hall, the murmurs of the banquet quieting the further they walked.

The magistrate's mansion was impeccably kept. The rock gardens were arranged artfully, the low shrubs well trimmed, and the verandas cleanly swept and polished. They stopped before the latticed double doors of a side room connected to the central wing.

Zhi Lan stood with her head lowered, her heart pounding and her cheeks flushed slightly from wine. She wondered what treasure Magistrate Bu spoke of. Were they going to see his legendary art collection?

She was so lost in her thoughts that she jumped when the magistrate spoke.

"Is this your student? What is her name?"

"Zhi Lan, my lord," Master Dan said. "She has been with me for about a year now."

"Indeed! Why does she cower so?" Magistrate Bu looked to her. "Do you speak, Miss Zhi Lan?"

"F-forgive me, my lord," Zhi Lan stammered. She hadn't expected to be addressed. Most people mistook her as a servant, and she was used to letting Master Dan do the talking. And she had to admit, speaking to a bureaucrat—especially a magistrate—made her break out in cold sweat. "This is all so extraordinary, I'm merely at a loss for words."

Magistrate Bu chuckled. "A lovely voice to go with a lovely face."

Zhi Lan smiled uncomfortably. She wished the magistrate could have praised her skill instead of her looks, as he did with Master Dan. There was merit to building a skill. There was no merit to how she looked—it wasn't as if she had carved her face herself. And yet, Zhi Lan knew the polite thing would be to smile and accept the compliment demurely.

So she did.

"You mustn't be afraid," Magistrate Bu said, leaning toward her. His voice lowered to a conspiratorial volume. "You may speak freely. This place is soon to become your home." There was an odd glint in his eyes, and he seemed to stare at her with keen interest.

Zhi Lan ducked her head. "Thank you, my lord."

"You were going to show us something, my lord?" Master Dan prompted.

"Ah, yes." Magistrate Bu straightened and Zhi Lan breathed a little easier. "I have an extensive collection of treasures, as you may have heard. I hope that your paintings will grace these walls in the coming months."

The magistrate threw open the double doors and stepped over the raised threshold.

Zhi Lan gaped at the room they entered. It was the size of a luxurious suite, filled with polished hexagonal shelves that displayed porcelain vases embellished with deep blue patterns, bronze statuettes, and exquisitely painted fans. Standing screens depicting dreamy mountain scenery were pushed against each wall. The scent of wood lacquer and paper lingered in the air, thick with artistic possibilities.

"Impressive!" Master Dan exclaimed. "How long have you been collecting?"

"Since I began studying for the imperial exams, twenty-five years ago. Art was like a balm to my soul back then. It still is now." Magistrate Bu assessed the room with unveiled pride. Zhi Lan felt she would be strutting like a peacock too if she had such a collection. "Let me tell you of my most recent acquisition. Two days ago my men came across something peculiar while hunting—an abandoned chest in the river, quite aged. I knew at once it contained great treasure."

Master Dan raised his white brows. "Indeed? What was inside?"

"Mud from the river and old peasants' clothes." The magistrate waved his hand in front of his nose as if the mere mention of those items stank. "I was almost about to throw it back in, but there was a box buried at the bottom. Inside was the most exquisite item."

What could possibly be more exquisite than the art already in the room? Zhi Lan was dying of curiosity, but she didn't say so. Master Dan must've sensed her eagerness, for he smiled and said, "Pray, do show us, my lord. You are keeping us in suspense."

Magistrate Bu gestured to his steward, who scampered off into the shelves, then came back with a small handheld scroll with silken ties. He unfurled it carefully.

Zhi Lan gasped.

It was a painting of a dragon done in loose, expressive brushstrokes. Its scaled body wove in and out of a cluster of swirling clouds like a winding river. It had a proud mane, great sapphire horns, and golden claws. The creature exuded pride and strength, but there was a playfulness to it too in the curved flick of its tail. It was so fluid and life-like that Zhi Lan almost thought she saw it move.

"Exquisite, is it not?" the magistrate boasted.

"Oh, yes!" Zhi Lan exclaimed, enraptured. "But where are the eyes?"

Two blank white orbs sat on the dragon's face. It was missing its irises. Zhi Lan thought it looked achingly incomplete without them. She noticed too that there was no inscription on the paper, and no red seal that indicated the artist's name.

"Therein lies the mystery," the magistrate said. "It is an unfinished work by an unknown master. It is a rare painting—one of a kind!"

Zhi Lan looked to Master Dan, who seemed to have been rendered speechless by the piece.

"A mystery indeed!" Master Dan said. "It's magnificent."

Magistrate Bu waved his steward away. Zhi Lan watched the servant disappear behind the shelves with the dragon painting, wishing she could look at the piece for a while longer.

"You will have access to this room as long as I am your patron," the magistrate said, clasping his hands behind his back. "Do you think this collection of mine is a significant source of inspiration, Li Chen? Will you be able to make many pieces of such quality for me?"

Master Dan bowed. "Of course, my lord! I have never been more delighted by a room in my life. You have provided me countless masters to learn from. May I take a look around?"

"Han, show Master Dan the bamboo scrolls," Magistrate Bu said, waving a hand at his steward, who scampered back to his side. "Miss Zhi Lan. You are welcome to explore as you please too."

"Thank you, my lord," Zhi Lan said. She made a move to follow Han and Master Dan, but Magistrate Bu stood in the way, a wet smile on his lips. She smiled back hesitantly, then turned on her heel to the other side of the room. Maybe she'd be able to find the dragon painting and study it a little more.

Han had put it away in the far corner, so that was where she would go.

Zhi Lan wandered past scrolls with calligraphy done in massive brushstrokes, delicate paintings of bamboo forests, and intricately enameled bronze containers. Scrolls overlapped on the walls and a vase concealed a delightful jade sculpture of a lion. Master Dan was right. This was a room of countless masters.

It was almost overwhelming. Zhi Lan wished each piece was given room to breathe and be admired.

She ducked into a narrow space where a large silk screen was half hidden behind a circular shelf. The silk was stretched over a polished wooden frame, embellished with gold gilding. At the top right corner was an inscription:

Lovers entwine beneath the willow boughs;
Like spring, passion blooms.

Zhi Lan sucked in a breath at the painting beneath. It depicted a man and a woman in front of a small pavilion beneath a willow tree. The lady was scantily dressed, her robe parted to expose the half moons of her breasts. The man embracing her was wearing nothing at all.

And between his legs was a rather...rude protrusion.

"This painting is called *Scenery of the Spring Palace*."

Zhi Lan jumped. Magistrate Bu emerged from behind her, crowding the corner even further.

"Oh," Zhi Lan said stupidly. Utterly mortified, she made an attempt to escape, but realized that the magistrate was yet again standing in the way of the only exit.

Zhi Lan wasn't a prude, by any means. She had grown up in a small village, where everyone bathed in the same river, sometimes at the same time. Naked bodies were just that—naked bodies. It was the context and intent in which they were viewed that changed things. And *lovers entwining beneath willow boughs* certainly changed things.

"It is one of my favorites," Magistrate Bu said, smiling his wet smile again. From this proximity, his teeth were quite long and stained yellow. "It is a shame I can't display it. My wife has rather modest sensibilities."

Zhi Lan returned his smile nervously. "May I ask who the artist is? The line work is exquisite."

The magistrate shrugged. "A court painter. He was known for his depictions of the emperor's harem. I'm a collector of his work, as you can see."

Zhi Lan turned around, only to be faced with another couple in flagrante delicto. The composition was all elegance and decadence. In any other context, she would have loved to study it, but with the magistrate's overpowering presence and long-toothed smile, she wished she were anywhere else but here. "Of course, my lord," she said, feeling her cheeks burn.

"There you go cowering again, Miss Zhi Lan," Magistrate Bu said. "You tremble like a flower."

Zhi Lan felt a prick of annoyance at the comparison. She was *not* a flower...never mind that her name was rather floral. If the magistrate had been a villager, she would've told him exactly what she thought of his advances. But Magistrate Bu was their patron, not to mention the most powerful man in the city. She couldn't possibly give him one of her put-downs. Besides, what if she had misread his intentions? He was a patron of art. A scholar-gentleman. A respected civil servant.

Sweat broke across her brow as the magistrate stepped closer. Her mind spun, wondering what she could do or say to make him stop.

Please, please, please let there be a distraction.

An ungodly crash sounded from the courtyard. Then, screams erupted.

Magistrate Bu jerked toward the noise. "What in the name of heaven is going on out there?"

Han and Master Dan emerged from the other side of the room. Zhi Lan seized this opportunity to escape, joining Master Dan at the entrance.

They all rushed to the courtyard to see what the matter was. The lanterns had been lit in the wake of the waning daylight, illuminating the space in a yellow glow. Zhi Lan felt dazed and shaky with relief. A distraction had come as soon as she wished it! It was almost like divine intervention.

All thoughts of deities vanished when a dark figure hurtled toward them, half of their face covered with a soot black scarf. Under their arm was a scroll. Zhi Lan recognized the blue and gold silk brocade—she had held it in her hands just moments ago.

"Master Dan, your painting!" she cried.

At this, the thief locked eyes with her. It was a man. From beneath two dark brows, a pair of parchment beige irises glowered at her—pale and empty as if the color had been leached out of them.

Zhi Lan shrank back. A demon!

"Thief!" Magistrate Bu bellowed. "Guards, grab him!"

No one came immediately. After a few delayed seconds, the magistrate's guards stumbled in, having clearly imbibed on spirits. In their bulky armor and spears, they were no match for the man in black, who sprinted across the court-yard like a lynx through a forest.

Then, in a mighty leap too swift to be human, the thief disappeared over the wall.

2

Yao was annoyed with him. This was nothing new.

Shao Qing sat a little apart from the rest of the thieves in the forest clearing, leaning against a thick stalk of bamboo. The others were gathered in a circle around a crackling fire, chortling and slapping each other's backs in boisterous celebration. In their midst, Yao shot him occasional glares between gulps of chrysanthemum wine.

Shao Qing figured the thief lord would take him aside for a heady lecture in a minute. He studied the duck leg in his bowl drenched in a rich, dark sauce. The dense meat tasted like ash in his mouth. Still, he ate.

Finally, a heavy hand landed on his shoulder. Shao Qing looked up to see Yao glowering at him from beneath bushy brows.

"A word, Brother Qing."

Shao Qing set his bowl down and rose slowly from his seat. The others carried on, too drunk on wine and their own egos to notice Yao and Shao Qing step behind a cluster of overgrown bamboo.

"Is there a problem?" Shao Qing asked, knowing full well that there was.

Yao's face was red and splotchy from the alcohol, but his words were sharp enough. "What were you thinking, exposing yourself so recklessly?" he demanded. "In a magistrate's manor, of all places! That man could have you hanged with a flick of his pinky finger!"

Shao Qing shrugged a shoulder. "I didn't get caught."

"Yet!" Yao bellowed.

"I never get caught."

Shao Qing had once slipped a jade bangle off an old woman's wrist without even rustling her sleeve. He had helped her up after she stumbled over a strategically placed twig. The *he tian* jade was warm in his palm before the old woman had finished thanking him. Yao had been impressed enough by that, lauding him as swift, decisive, and steady. It was the theft that had earned him a spot in the gang.

"*You* never get caught but someday you'll get *us* caught," Yao said. "You're too reckless. Too cocky. Magistrate Bu may be a poor thief catcher, but you cannot count on his short-comings to protect yourself."

Shao Qing had yet to have his abilities proven wrong, so he said nothing.

Yao pointed a meaty finger at him. "Everyone else has the sense to listen to me and follow caution. We do this to build a life for ourselves. This is all we petty thieves have! What's important to you, Brother Qing? Chasing the next high? Provoking ill-fortune and slipping away again just because you can?"

Shao Qing's gaze drifted past Yao's shoulder. These days the bamboo forest looked more gray than green.

It's getting worse, he thought. He supposed he should've been alarmed, but even that had deserted him.

Yao made an irritated noise. "Is there a single thought in that brain of yours?"

"Apologies. I was distracted."

The thief lord shook his head. "Magistrate Bu's manor. Honestly! You're lucky that painting you took already has an interested buyer. We can't hold onto it for much longer if we want to keep our necks."

Shao Qing clasped his hands and bowed. "You work impressively fast, Elder Brother Yao." He knew the man was easily placated by respect and praise, if not proper remorse. Shao Qing was not feeling particularly remorseful.

It had been far too easy to infiltrate Magistrate Bu's manor during his banquet. His guards were careless, their senses dulled by celebratory drink, gone soft with the idea that no one would dare steal from the city magistrate. The entire gang had gone over the walls with no misstep. It would've been too routine to stay under Yao's cautious command. Shao Qing would've been numb to the entire heist.

Snatching the painting from the magistrate's own banquet table before an audience of shocked spectators had made his heart race and heat flood his veins. Shao Qing had felt weightless, like an immortal floating on clouds, as if something had awakened within him when he passed those manor gates.

"If you jeopardize us again, I'll have no choice but to kill you," Yao said darkly. "I have children to feed, for heaven's sake!"

It was an empty threat and they both knew it. He punched Shao Qing's shoulder and rejoined the group.

Yao was an odd combination of sentimental father and hardened criminal. He often liked to moralize about respect and filial piety, as if he were the head of a wealthy household instead of a group of immoral riff raff who would do anything for coin.

Some of the thieves were like him and had relatives to feed, but the rest were exactly what Yao thought Shao Qing was—youths who indulged in vice and recklessness for the sake of it. They were wasting their lives, whereas Shao Qing's had already been wasted.

He rubbed his shoulder—the pain had already dulled—and headed back to the clearing where the rest of the thieves sat. Their black robes were stark against the blazing fire in the center.

"Eat well, brothers!" Yao called out, already in a better mood. "We've earned it tonight!"

The men cheered.

As Shao Qing returned to his seat, someone sidled up to him.

"How do you do it, Brother Qing? Jump in like that without a care?" Wei asked breathlessly, his too-large eyes glimmering with awe. He was the youngest in the gang, no more than fifteen and as skinny as a mantis. "I thought that stunt was going to land you in prison!"

Shao Qing swallowed a bite of duck with some difficulty. "It was unwise," he said, feeling Yao glaring at him again.

"He is utterly fearless!" Xuan Bo, a stocky, middle-aged thief exclaimed.

The others cheered. Shao Qing forced a smile, though the corners of his lips felt stiff.

"So, did you get a little dragon for your collection this time?" Wei asked.

Nan You, a wiry thief with a dark goatee, hiccuped. "No one wants to see your little dragon, Shao Qing!"

The group guffawed uproariously.

"I did not," Shao Qing said shortly.

Wei sighed. "That's too bad. You could've had the coin to treat us to more wine."

"With the amount of art Brother Qing has stolen he should be rolling in gold," Xuan Bo interjected. "How much have you sold those pieces for?"

Shao Qing picked up his duck again. They had never asked him so many questions before. Despite having traveled together for three years, the other men still found him unsettling. He supposed it was his apathetic nature and his pale eyes. Demon's eyes, Yao had called them. He wasn't entirely wrong.

"I don't sell them," Shao Qing said. He was fine living off the wages Yao gave them from their collective heists, but he had a habit of snagging any painting with a dragon on it if it caught his eye. The art itself was worthless to him. Some he put back, others he threw into the river or dropped in the streets. None of them were ever what he thought they'd be.

Wei gaped at him. "Could it be that you actually *admire* the art, Brother Qing?"

"What's so unusual about that?" Yao snapped. "We should have appreciation for the things we sell. The better we know the subject, the better we can assess their value."

"But why have a rotten piece of paper when you can have gold?" Nan You complained. "I'd rather have a feast every day and Peony Pagoda songbirds on each arm than a dusty scroll on my wall."

"Then you're a prime idiot!" Yao slurred his words, having had several more gulps of chrysanthemum wine. He fumbled with the scroll at his belt and unrolled it, exposing the painting Shao Qing had stolen. "See here. An excellent mountain and river piece by an up and coming scholar painter. Exquisite brushwork, exquisite composition. I could just...*dive* right into this waterfall!" Yao made a swooping motion with his hand. "There aren't many paintings like this. This has a *freshness* to it, like a spiraled orange peel!"

"Brother Yao, I think you've had too much to drink."

The others murmured their assent, their attention now removed from Shao Qing. Wei, however, still lingered.

The boy withdrew a fruit from his sleeve. "I saved you a peach. You didn't take one earlier."

"I'm not hungry."

Wei shrugged and bit into the peach, juice dribbling down his chin as he peered at Shao Qing's bowl. "Are you going to finish that, then?"

He shook his head and offered the rest of the duck to Wei. It had since grown cold, and he was hardly tempted to finish food that tasted like cold, slimy ash.

Wei took a large bite into the meat and groaned. "This is good stuff! They know how to make it right in the South Street Market." He chewed and swallowed. "Do you not like duck, Brother Qing?"

He did, once.

The sound of booted feet hitting the earth made Shao Qing pause. Spots of yellow torchlight flickered to life at the forest line.

"Drat." Yao stood unsteadily. "The constables are here."

The gang scrambled to their feet. Someone raked dirt over the fire, plunging the clearing into darkness.

"Do you reckon they're looking for us?" Wei squeaked.

"Of course they are," Yao whispered harshly. The proximity to danger seemed to sober him. "The magistrate sent them."

Shao Qing couldn't see, but he figured the thief lord was shooting an accusatory glare at him.

"What do we do? Go to headquarters?"

The abandoned building they congregated in was only a mile from the forest. It was too close, too obvious.

"No. Everyone, scatter. If they catch one of us they catch all of us," Yao said darkly. "Go!"

Footfalls rustled the forest floor, then, nothing. It was good they were all light-footed—but whether they were good at hiding was another thing. Shao Qing assessed the torches. He could go deeper into the forest and wait, or he could pass the guards without detection. They wouldn't expect a thief to go back into the city.

So that's exactly what Shao Qing did.

NIGHT LIFE IN ZHU CITY was limited to the outskirts where the poor and middle class dwelt. Tea houses, shops, restaurants, and brothels towered over the stall-lined streets. Shao Qing passed the restaurant on the South Street Market where they had purchased the duck, its tiled eaves dangling with red paper lanterns. It lay before the foot of the massive bridge that connected the outer wards of the city to the inner wards where the wealthy were situated.

On either side of the bridge, vendors hollered their wares behind stalls. Hawthorn fruits gleamed on skewers, glazed in hard sugar shells. The smoky scent of green onion pancakes and other street food was thick in the hazy air. People bustled past, chattering and shouting, as children ran underfoot, kicking a tasseled ball between the feet of passersby.

Shao Qing kept his gaze on the paved ground as he crossed, weaving through the crowd at a leisurely pace so as to not arouse suspicion. He would have to find somewhere in the city to hide. But where?

The noises and crowd faded as he approached the opposite end of the bridge. When the high walls of the courtyard houses came into view, Shao Qing was struck with a thought. It was true the constables wouldn't expect him to return to the city, but they would expect even less that he would return to the scene of the crime so soon.

Offending a magistrate was a hefty felony. Anyone with a healthy dose of fear would stay away.

The ward gate loomed before the end of the bridge, manned by two guards on either side. It towered two stories high, separating the rich from the rest of the city. Only the wealthy or tradesmen on official business could pass through freely—heaven forbid a lowly carp jump over the dragon's gate.

Shao Qing turned left into an alleyway between the gate and another building before the guards spotted him, running his hand along the rough wall. At the very end was a gap just big enough for a person to slip through undetected. He did so now, wedging himself through the uneven stone and emerging on the other side. It was a good thing the gate was severely understaffed.

He wove through cleanly swept streets until he stood beneath Magistrate Bu's manor. The west wall was grown over with strong, flourishing vines to conceal a crumbling hole at the foot of it. The magistrate's vanity was the precise reason Yao was able to find a way into the manor.

Shao Qing braced his foot against the wall and began to climb.

One of the benefits of his condition was that his inner stillness manifested outwardly. Fear and hesitation made thieves stumble—Shao Qing never stumbled. His limbs were steady even as some of the vines pulled loose and the rough stone scraped his knuckles. The journey up the wall was swift. He landed silently on the tiled roof and crouched beside a row of guardian statues that lined the ridge, hoping his silhouette blended in with the stone creatures.

This was the front section of the west wing where Shao Qing figured the magistrate housed his servants. People of less importance were always placed away from the inner courtyard, which meant there was less security here. The room beneath him had a dim light that shone through a latticed wooden door. A pair of plain shoes were set by the entry, small and dainty. A maidservant, perhaps. Someone he could easily overpower.

Shao Qing peered over the raised lip of the eaves. No guards.

He leapt down and slipped silently into the room.

THE AUDACITY! THE DISRESPECT! I'll have that good for nothing thief hanged at the city gate!" Magistrate Bu's face was as purple as a plum.

Master Dan and Zhi Lan sat awkwardly in the main hall, their heads lowered as the servants stood by in fearful silence. The parlor was lit by lanterns. Spots of yellow light reflected on the polished wooden floor, blinking out when the magistrate stormed over them in a swirl of dark robes.

"Calm down, my lord," Lady Bu said in a placating tone. "The constables will find him in due time."

"What do you know, woman?" Magistrate Bu spat, waving his hand as if his wife was a pesky fly. He resumed pacing, scowling at the maidservant who entered to bring in a tray of tea. She cowered and scampered away.

Zhi Lan couldn't believe how quickly things went south. Not thirty minutes ago she'd been admiring the courtyard and dreaming of a promising future.

"*My* manor, broken into by a common thief!" Magistrate Bu threw his arms down, the fabric of his massive sleeves snapping harshly behind him. "My masterpiece, gone!"

Master Dan clasped his hands respectfully as he addressed the magistrate. "If I may be so bold to say, my lord, it is only a painting. I am more than capable of creating another piece for you, as many as you desire as long as I am under your patronage."

Magistrate Bu narrowed his eyes. A dangerous sort of silence pervaded the room. The hairs on the back of Zhi Lan's neck stood up.

"This isn't about you, Li Chen," the magistrate hissed. "I have shown that painting to everyone of importance. They will expect me to have it back. How can I let a mere *thief* cheat me?"

Zhi Lan wasn't overly familiar with the ways of officials, but she knew that a magistrate was meant to enforce justice and arrest thieves and robbers. If they were unable to catch a criminal, it would be a demerit, a mark on their record. If they failed frequently, they would be dismissed.

Magistrate Bu was not only risking losing face. He was risking his position.

Master Dan bowed again. "Surely, my lord, it is no fault of your own—"

"I intend to have that painting back, one way or another," Magistrate Bu said. "You will make me a duplicate. I will give you three days."

Zhi Lan glanced up, startled. Master Dan looked at a loss for words.

"What's this? Are you hesitating?"

Master Dan bowed. "It's an unusual request, for those in my line of work, my lord. I am not a commercial painter. Furthermore, the original took me three months on site. I have no doubt that your lordship will be able to find the thief—"

"I have paid and provided for you, Dan Li Chen. If you can't copy a mere painting you can hang with that thief for all I care!"

Zhi Lan froze. Surely the magistrate wasn't serious.

"As you wish, my lord. My student and I will begin working immediately," Master Dan said evenly.

"Get out of my sight," the magistrate snarled.

With a low bow, Master Dan took Zhi Lan's arm and hurried out the hall.

ZHI LAN'S HEART WAS STILL pounding by the time the servants guided them into their rooms. They were housed in the west wing of Magistrate Bu's massive courtyard manor. Both of them had a lavishly furnished suite to themselves, but Zhi Lan followed Master Dan into his, bracing herself for a sleepless night. The magistrate's threat rung in her ears, making her sick to her stomach. She couldn't help but feel partially responsible. After all, hadn't she prayed for a distraction? Some passing immortal must have granted her wish. Or more likely a mischievous spirit, considering the circumstances.

But it wouldn't do to admit this to Master Dan. Especially not if she had to reveal the reason she wanted the distraction in the first place.

No, it was better to keep *that* to herself.

"I suppose we should begin," Master Dan said with a sigh.

He seated himself at a mahogany table supplied with paper, brushes, and an inkstone. Zhi Lan went to light the candles.

The room was far larger than any room she'd stayed in before, with a study area on a raised platform, a sitting area, and a sleeping area complete with an alcove bed. She would've loved to explore the place if she weren't so anxious.

Master Dan gestured to his trunks which were set before the desk. "The silk."

Zhi Lan retrieved a bolt of plain white silk, unrolling it to the appropriate length. They worked in silence, cutting the silk to size, then priming it with a liquid mixture of glue and alum with a wide brush. They then spread it on a board, waiting for the sticky substance to dry—only then would the silk be ready to take ink. Zhi Lan had been fascinated when Master Dan first showed her this process. She had done it many times since. Now, she found some comfort in its ritualistic familiarity.

Master Dan regarded the drying silk with a contemplative air. The only sign of his distress was the deep crease between his white brows.

"Shall we try it on paper first?" Zhi Lan piped up. "I think I remember the composition well enough."

He dipped his head in acquiescence.

Silk paintings usually started with a line drawing on paper. The artist would then place the primed silk on top and trace over the drawing with a fine brush. But Master Dan had felt spontaneous on the day they went to Shui Jin Mountain, so he painted directly on the silk. As a result, there was no paper sketch that he could retrace. They really had to start from scratch.

Zhi Lan and Master Dan each took a sheet of paper from beneath a hefty paperweight. She dribbled some water into the inkstone beside it and began to grind with an ink stick. After a few moments of silence, broken only by the steady scraping of the inkstone, Master Dan took a brush and soaked its white bristles into the dark well.

"Well, my dear disciple, what do you think of this situation we've gotten ourselves into?" Master Dan said at last.

"Earning Magistrate Bu's patronage? I think it's an achievement, sir," Zhi Lan said politely.

"You know what I'm speaking of."

Zhi Lan rubbed her chin. "Very well. It's terrible and we're doomed."

Master Dan laughed. "An accurate description." He grew serious again, hovering his brush over the paper. "Is this what you want, child? To follow me city to city and work under the whims of bureaucrats?"

Master Dan was from an impoverished noble family that had fallen from grace after his late father had gambled away all their riches. He had cut ties with his family completely, opting for a nomadic artist's life, living off one patron to another.

"Of course! I wouldn't have begged for your tutelage otherwise," Zhi Lan said.

She didn't think that was such a bad life to live. She had first met Master Dan over a year ago, when she was still living in a remote farming village with her parents and broth-ers. He had been a traveler, seeking a great river to paint. Ma had taken one look at his white scholar's robes and deemed him respectable enough to offer him temporary lodging. Zhi Lan had been endlessly curious—and delighted—to find that Master Dan was a painter. She was exceedingly fond of drawing herself, though she never had enough pa-per to indulge the hobby.

Master Dan had offered his supplies to let Zhi Lan demonstrate her skill. She had drawn one of her chickens, Pu'er, with black ink. Master Dan had subsequently let her use his colored pigments, which Zhi Lan dipped her brushes into eagerly, resulting in a chicken with ultramarine blue and cinnabar red feathers, though Pu'er was a primarily brown chicken.

"Overzealous with ink, perhaps, but a steady hand and a good sense of composition," Master Dan had concluded. He had then let Zhi Lan look through his portfolio, which in-cluded a half-finished painting of a rocky landscape.

"I am looking for a river to go here," Master Dan had said, tapping the empty bottom half of the painting. "Will you help me find one?"

The next day was the first of their many grand nature excursions. Zhi Lan had led Master Dan to the neighboring river they used to irrigate the farm. The current was strong that morning, throwing white foam against the rocks. She had helped Master Dan grind his inks and hovered over his shoulder as he created magic before her very eyes.

By evening, she had practically begged on her knees for him to accept her as his student.

Zhi Lan was brought back to the present when Master Dan sighed and set down his brush with a click. His paper was unmarked.

"I can't help but think you're meant to find your fortune elsewhere," Master Dan said. He gestured to the lavish apartments around them. "This is an old bachelor's life. I travel and paint to make a name for myself. I bend to the whims of my patrons. I have these rooms, but depend on another to provide them to me. Zhi Lan, you are young. This is as good a time as any to return home and get married. I won't blame you if you leave."

Magistrate Bu's threat lingered over them, heavy yet unspoken.

"If I marry, I will have to bend to the whims of my husband and depend on him to provide my rooms. The situation isn't much of an alternative, is it?" Zhi Lan said with a wry smile. "I'd much rather suffer with you, if I have to suffer at all. Besides, there is still much you need to teach me."

Master Dan tsked. "Someone ought to teach you to curb that smart mouth of yours."

"They can try."

He didn't laugh. "I'm getting old. I worry I will have nothing to leave you. No name, no legacy. Will you promise to go home after I'm gone, child? I don't want you wandering about in this manner alone."

"Master Dan, please don't speak of such things!" Zhi Lan cried. "You have decades left to live. That's plenty of time to make a name for yourself and turn this situation of ours around. We'll solve this together."

Master Dan merely sighed.

Zhi Lan picked up the brush he had set down, rewetted it with ink, and hovered the tip over her paper. "It was like this, yes?" She swept her brush upward, tracing the towering contour of Shui Jin Mountain.

IT WAS NEARING MIDNIGHT WHEN Zhi Lan retired to her room, setting her shoes outside and donning her indoor slippers. The suite was connected to Master Dan's and equally nice, featuring lush furniture and a vanity with a large bronze mirror. Pots of cosmetics were arranged on the table. She didn't presume they were for her use, but she did peek in the red enameled containers out of curiosity before changing for bed and pulling the pins from her hair.

The alcove bed was covered in sky blue sheets, so large that she could roll over twice. It was a luxury compared to her own straw sleeping pallet at home and the hard, narrow beds of tea houses. Zhi Lan sighed, grateful at least for the promising comfort of a cozy night's sleep.

After washing up with a basin of water, she sat before the mirror and began to comb her hair.

Before Master Dan had dismissed her, Zhi Lan attempted a few sketches of his Shui Jin Mountain painting. She couldn't be sure if any of the iterations were correct, as Master Dan hadn't commented on them. He had only thanked her for her efforts and told her to reconvene tomorrow.

She recalled the very first lesson Master Dan had taught her on her first day as his disciple. "Everything we paint must have a deeper meaning," he had said. "There is symbolism to be found in every composition, in every rock, bird, and tree. To paint is to communicate. If one has nothing to say, there is no purpose in picking up a brush."

With Shui Jin Mountain, Master Dan had wanted to capture the grand mysticism of the waterfall, juxtaposing the serenity of their early morning surroundings by the sheer power of the falls in the distance. He had captured an ephemeral moment.

Painting a mere replica went against the very reason Master Dan made art.

Zhi Lan was perturbed by his somber attitude and his talk of growing old and passing on. Death was on his mind. With the magistrate's threat, she couldn't blame him. But Zhi Lan was determined to help him turn this around. She wanted him to succeed. And selfishly, she didn't want to go back home yet.

Her comb snagged in her hair. Zhi Lan frowned, staring at her reflection. The glimpses she had caught of herself in the past were always in pools of water, where the ripples distorted her features. She was dismayed to find that her shoulders were narrower than she thought they were, so unlike her brothers' broad ones, as if a strong gust of wind could knock her over.

Ba used to joke that he had found her outside a rich family's manor.

"My little orchid looks more like a lady than a farm girl," he'd say to her affectionately. "Perhaps you are meant for greater things, Lan'er."

Greater things. Like marriage.

Zhi Lan was nearing twenty. If she went back now, she knew her family would nudge her toward a match. Their farm was struggling, barely recovered from the previous years of drought and failed crops. Well-off in-laws would be a massive help. Yet she hated the idea of making her fortune by marrying.

She wanted to support her family like her brothers did—through her own hard work—even if she knew she wasn't useful on the farm in the way they were.

The only reason Ma and Ba had consented to Zhi Lan leaving with Master Dan was because he was kind enough not to charge tuition like a formal school would. Free education wasn't something to pass up.

Zhi Lan eyed the ornamented containers on the vanity hesitantly, then plucked off the lid of a tin enameled with a peony. Within lay small rectangular sheets of vermilion-tinted paper. She wet her lips and brought a sheet between them, pressing gently.

Her reflection stared back with a red mouth. She had seen the girls in her village before their wedding processions, dressed in their best robes, their lips painted just like this beneath red veils.

A painted face was art, too. Just not the sort Zhi Lan preferred.

She capped the tin and rubbed her lips, suddenly not recognizing herself. The color was stubborn, however, and remained too bold and too vibrant on her skin.

Things like this always brought unwanted attention.

She looked away from the mirror and focused on working the snag out of her hair, a frown furrowing her brow. Color, like beauty, faded. Skill could only grow.

A loud thump sounded from the roof. Zhi Lan jumped, dropping her comb with a clack. She waited a second, then two. Silence. Slowly, she let herself relax. Perhaps it was just a loose branch that had fallen.

Zhi Lan tossed her hair back and padded past the silk screen that separated the sleeping area from the sitting area, intending to blow out the dim candle on the table.

She did not expect to run headfirst into a tall, shadowed mass.

Zhi Lan gasped and stumbled back.

A man loomed over her, dressed in black from the toes of his scuffed boots to the scarf tied around the lower half of his face.

"Don't scream," the man said.

Zhi Lan screamed.

And was abruptly cut off when a large hand clamped over her mouth. An arm banded around her waist and lifted her from the ground. Zhi Lan struggled, gagging when she managed to inhale through his fingers. Skies, was that dirt and duck grease?

The man dumped her unceremoniously into her alcove bed, looming over the entrance so there was no escape. Zhi Lan scrambled to the corner, half frozen in fear. She managed to pelt him with her slipper. It bounced off his chest harmlessly.

"W-Who are you? What do you want?" she choked out.

"Be quiet and nothing will happen to you," the man said. He had a surprisingly smooth voice. No doubt a trick to make her let her guard down.

Zhi Lan's mind jumped to the magistrate's threat. "Did Magistrate Bu hire you? I-I don't want to die, I didn't do anything wrong! My master and I are working on the painting as we speak. I promise we'll—"

He climbed onto the bed, clamping his hand over her mouth again, and pinned her to the far wall with his body, his limbs hard and unyielding.

Zhi Lan squeaked, her eyes watering both from fear and his stench. Through the blur of her tears, she caught sight of his eyes. Pale, parchment beige with stark black pupils. Terrible demon's eyes that she'd recognize anywhere.

It was the dirty thief who had stolen Master Dan's painting.

Anger replaced her fear. Then, she was struck with a stupid thought. The thief in his horrible, dusty thieves' clothes was on her *clean bed*, boots and all! How dare he!

"Hmmmph!" Zhi Lan said.

And skies, his fingers stank! Her brothers used to mess with her in the same way, pressing their dirty hands over her nose and mouth after they had spent hours doing farm work. Regretfully, there was only one way to repel them.

Without thinking, Zhi Lan stuck out her tongue and licked the thief's palm.

"What are you—?"

He retracted his hand, scrunching his eyebrows as he stared at the shiny spot of saliva on his skin.

Zhi Lan spat the salty, greasy taste out of her mouth and gasped for air, though she only got a lungful of the thief's scent, as he still hadn't let go of her. He smelled like forest and sweat and smoke. And that horrible duck grease again. "Apologize!"

He stared.

"Apologize...right...now. This is no way to treat a woman, you horrible, smelly criminal!"

To her embarrassment, tears blurred her vision once more and her shoulders began to shake with sobs. She was tired and hungry and certainly did *not* want to fight for her life at the moment. Of course it was just her luck to have the thief who had started this series of unfortunate events come to her room and rob her of a good night's rest along with everything else in her life.

"I...apologize. Please stop crying."

The thief slowly released her and sat back on the bed, settling his hands on his knees. He was still blocking her escape, but at least he wasn't manhandling her anymore. His eyes were terrifying, but they held no expression. No anger, no desire. They were strangely...blank.

Zhi Lan sniffled and wiped her eyes with her sleeves, unsure of what to make of this strange turn of events.

"What's your name?" the thief said.

"N-Nong Zhi Lan."

He nodded slowly. "A farmer's name."

"It is." She swallowed and hugged her knees to her chest. "Are you here to steal more? I-I ought to call the guards on you."

Those blank eyes studied her. "Tell me, Miss Nong, why does it matter to you if a rich magistrate becomes a little less rich?"

Zhi Lan raised her chin. If he was willing to philosophize with her, perhaps he possessed *some* gentlemanly qualities. "It doesn't," she said. "But my master and I are under Magistrate Bu's patronage. That painting you stole is the sole reason we're here. His lordship intended to add it to his collection. And now that it's gone, he's threatening to *hang* us! This is all your fault!"

Then she'd be dead. Or if Master Dan found some way to save her, she'd have to go back to her parents in the village with nothing to show for her efforts. Her brothers would tease her relentlessly for her failed pursuits and she'd be a burden to Ma and Ba. She'd be too weak to be useful around the farm and too proud to make money by any other means but her own. She'd mourn Master Dan and wish she could've done something for him—anything.

This miserable train of thought brought fresh tears to her eyes.

"I don't see how the magistrate's bad temper is my fault," the thief said.

Zhi Lan scowled. Perhaps he was not so gentlemanly after all. "We might die without that painting!"

The thief blinked slowly. "Then you ought to find a more practical line of work."

Her face heated. "You're one to talk, you petty thief!"

"Mine is a lucrative field," he said calmly. "What good are artists and scholars? You wear the same white robes and wax poetic about ridiculous things. A painting from one master is indistinguishable from the next. You paint the same mountains, the same birds. You find meaning where there is none. At the end of the day, art is for thieves like me to profit from, and for the rich to feel superior."

Zhi Lan grabbed her other slipper and flung it at him.

4

THE SHOE SMACKED THE SIDE of Shao Qing's head. He didn't move, though the blow rather smarted.

"You...you!" the girl sputtered. "I've never heard such drivel in my life!"

He had expected to run into a maidservant, but somehow it ended up being her—the apprentice of that old painter.

She was a strangely hyper one, this Nong Zhi Lan, gasping and sputtering and kicking as if she had the energy of a thousand wild birds. Shao Qing should've drugged her with his handkerchief ages ago. And yet, here they were conversing.

From this proximity, he assessed her figure. She was too slender to be fashionably beautiful, but she had a good head of hair and all her teeth. Her features were delicate, comparable to the most sought after courtesans in The Peony Pagoda. Her eyes were wide, her lashes wet from her earlier episode. Her lips were especially perfect. Full and shockingly red, with a symmetrical cupid's bow.

They pressed into a harsh, thin line.

Shao Qing's breath caught.

Strange! He wondered at his reaction. What had it been? Her beauty? Surely not. Shao Qing had come across plenty of pretty girls and he hadn't felt any which way about them. There was something different about her—or about this place—that made him more aware of himself. For once he didn't feel completely numb. He felt...awake. Just like he had when he stole the magistrate's painting.

Shao Qing brought his gaze back to the girl's eyes. She glared at him fiercely.

"If you're worried about your prospects," he said slowly, "the magistrate will keep you whether you paint or not."

She caught his meaning easily enough. Miss Nong drew herself up to her full diminutive height while still remaining seated. "How dare you! You are the rudest, most rotten, most addle-brained *egg* I've ever had the displeasure of speaking to! Didn't your mother teach you any manners?"

A bubble of amusement ran up his throat. Amusement! Shao Qing was compelled to crack a smile, though it was concealed beneath his mask. "I have no mother."

Movement sounded outside—the shuffling of footsteps and the deep voices of guards.

Shao Qing turned, alert.

Such a range of feelings tonight, he mused.

It wasn't entirely unwelcome. And neither was the light that shone through the latticed doors, silhouetting the approaching guards. He didn't know how he'd been spotted, but getting out of a scrape was one of his favorite pastimes.

Shao Qing scanned the room. It was an open planned suite, the sleeping area, sitting area, and study each sectioned off by a silk screen. The space was sparsely furnished. There was nowhere to hide.

He turned back to Miss Nong. "I don't suppose there's another way out?"

"I'll tell the guards you're here," she choked out.

Surely the chit wasn't threatening him.

"I'll tell the guards unless you promise to return my master's painting."

"You're in no position to make bargains, little girl."

"I am not a little girl!"

Shao Qing held up his hand, his palm still moist from when she had licked it before. She scowled.

A harsh knock sounded at the door, the wooden frame rattling. "Open up. There's an intruder on the loose."

A triumphant gleam shone in Miss Nong's eyes.

Before Shao Qing could stop her, she cupped her hands around her mouth. "Coming!"

Miss Nong smoothed the front of her robe and leaned back against the wall, a satisfied smirk playing at the edge of her perfect lips. "Well, thief? Make your choice."

Shao Qing was aware of his blood rushing to his ears. And his heartbeat pounding faster. This was the thrill that came to him when he was at the threshold of trouble. It was glorious.

He was vaguely aware that if he did get caught, he'd spend the rest of his days behind bars. He could go completely numb in captivity—there would be no thieving to make his blood rush in prison. Perhaps he'd lose consciousness altogether and become a vegetable. The possibility was always at the periphery. An inevitable fate worse than death. And then death itself. There was still a conscious part of him that feared it.

Which meant he would have to accept this girl's bargain. For now.

"Fine," Shao Qing said.

There was an impatient knock at the door. "What's going on in there?"

Miss Nong cupped a hand to her ear. "Fine what?"

So she liked to gloat. Shao Qing felt that bubble of amusement again. "Fine, I'll return your master's painting."

She nodded, then threw her bed covers over his head. "Hide."

Shao Qing obeyed, laying himself down.

The patter of feet and the sound of the door creaking open was muffled by the blankets.

"So sorry," Miss Nong said with a stifled yawn. "I had just gone to bed. Did you say there was an intruder on the loose?"

"Yes. A man dressed in black. Have you noticed any movement, any suspicious noises?"

"I'm afraid not."

"We were instructed to search every room. If you don't mind, miss?"

"Oh yes, search as you please," Miss Nong said calmly. She was an impressive actress, he'd give her that. "I'll be off to bed, if *you* don't mind. It's dreadfully late."

"Er...I don't think that's—"

"I must run an early errand for my master tomorrow. He needs supplies to replicate the painting that dirty thief stole. The faster my master finishes the painting the sooner Magistrate Bu will be happy. I reckon you don't want to keep his lordship unhappy?"

"Of course not, miss."

"Carry on then," Miss Nong said. Light footsteps came closer. The bedclothes were lifted for a fraction of a second, then the girl threw herself on top of him and covered them both with the blankets.

The wind was knocked out of Shao Qing, but he slowly inhaled even as his face was suffocated by Miss Nong's shoulder.

She smelled faintly of jasmine soap and pu'er tea. It was a pleasant scent. Shao Qing found himself inhaling deeper. He couldn't remember the last time he had smelled something nice so acutely.

They stayed there for a good few minutes as the magistrate's guards searched the room, the silence punctuated by occasional thumps. A pair of footsteps sounded closer.

"That will be all, miss," the guard said from somewhere at the head of the bed.

Miss Nong gave a sleepy grunt. Shao Qing imagined she looked quite comfortable on the outside, belly down and cocooned in a generous mass of blankets.

In reality, most of that mass was him, and her limbs were tangled awkwardly with his. The late spring heat made the air stifling. She was all sharp elbows and knees. One of which was jabbing into his sternum most uncomfortably.

It felt like an eternity before the footsteps faded and the doors creaked shut. Miss Nong finally removed herself, releasing Shao Qing from the suffocating bedding. He sucked in a breath of air.

"Did they feed you chicken feed on the farm?" He rubbed the sore spot on his sternum.

Miss Nong's face twisted in confusion. "No, I had rice like everyone else." Then she mumbled something under her breath that sounded very much like, "Skies, is he crazy too?"

She straightened her clothes and sat back, watching him as he stood from the bed.

"Much thanks. I'm afraid I've disturbed you long enough." He clasped his hands and bowed, then turned to the door.

"Sleep here tonight."

Shao Qing turned back and raised a brow at the slight, rumpled figure on the bed. "I'm flattered, Miss Nong. But I'm afraid I'm not interested."

"I don't mean *that,* you scoundrel! How do I know you'll keep your promise and return Master Dan's painting?" she demanded.

She wouldn't. Because he had no intention of keeping that promise. He didn't know where her master's painting had gone, and even with his newfound range of feelings, he realized he didn't care. Yao had taken off with it. And knowing how efficient the thief lord was, it would be sold first thing in the morning.

"I gave you my word," Shao Qing said.

"The word of a thief means little."

Shao Qing considered his options. Either way, the girl had no power over him, despite what she may think. He could agree to stay but sneak out in the middle of the night. Or he could stay in earnest and see through the bargain.

In a span of a few minutes, Shao Qing had felt more than he had felt in years. There was something about Miss Nong that affected him. Perhaps he was close to his soul. And perhaps she'd be able to lead him to it. It was an intriguing prospect, even if he didn't care too much for the end result. He was not opposed to an adventure, seeing as Yao and the gang would likely be lying low for some weeks. Besides, he was tired of running. At least for tonight.

He nodded. "Very well. Where do I sleep?"

SHAO QING SLEPT ON THE floor. Despite the warm evening, Miss Nong had bundled up in her bed until she resembled a lump more than a girl before saying a brusque good night.

The floor was hard and Miss Nong hadn't given him a pillow, but at least he had somewhere secure to stay until the morning.

Shao Qing closed his eyes and dreamed the same dream he had for six years.

He was a dragon. His scales shimmered gold, his claws gleaming a deep sapphire blue. Through soft, hazy vision, Shao Qing saw his tail sink into an open scroll. Silk. He struggled to move, but a dark, suffocating force sucked him in, compressing his body into line and ink. He only caught sight of a gilded scroll rod before darkness pressed down on him. Then he stayed there, sightless and frozen. Aware, yet unable to move.

Shao Qing knew the dream would go on that way, a night of infinite numbness.

But tonight, the dragon writhed and twisted between painted clouds.

Z HI LAN HAD A FITFUL sleep, spending half the night wondering if she had gone mad inviting a criminal to her room. It was some time before dawn when she woke, the room shrouded in a soft, intimate sort of dimness. After making sure there was no movement from her guest, she peeked over the side of her bed. He resembled nothing more than a black mass on the floor, his chest rising and falling with even breaths.

Thank heavens he didn't snore.

The thief had agreed to the sleeping arrangement easily enough. It was *her* bed after all, and she had rights to it, even if he had soiled it with his dirty criminal clothes. But she swore that he had *sniffed* her while they were hiding from the guards. Zhi Lan had expected him to charm and wheedle her into sharing a bed as befitting of an irritating man.

Instead he had laid himself on the floor, tucked his hands behind his head, and went to sleep without a word.

That should have relieved her, but it only made her more suspicious. Who *was* this thief? He was a scoundrel, a gentleman, and a criminal rolled into one. Polite yet impolite. Honorable yet dishonorable. He was wholly unpredictable, and that was dangerous.

Zhi Lan squinted. He slept with his mask still on, the lower half of his face a complete mystery. The upper half was nice enough, she supposed, when he wasn't staring with those unsettling eyes of his. He had straight, elegant brows and high cheekbones. And the hint of a tall nose bridge.

What if he really was a demon? Had she damned herself and her entire family by associating with him? She shuddered. Even if it were so, he couldn't be more dangerous than an angry magistrate. And if she were damned, at least it was for the sake of their livelihoods.

Just as the room began to lighten, Zhi Lan slipped out of bed and threw on her outer robe and yesterday's skirt. She ducked past the silk screen that separated the sleeping area from the sitting area of her chamber, already overrun with nerves.

She wasn't sure if she was important enough to be served, but a maidservant might enter at any moment and was bound to notice a man in her room, if only by smell alone. Zhi Lan wrinkled her nose as she breathed a little deeper. The thief utterly stank up the place with his odor, when before it had smelled like fresh soap and jasmine.

He *had* promised to return Master Dan's painting, but she wasn't about to let him out of her sight.

Which meant Zhi Lan would have to go with him today.

After rummaging around for paper and ink, she penned a quick note to Master Dan.

Master,

I have gone to the market this morning to purchase paint. I noticed you were running low on the brown pigment you like to use. I will be back much later, as I have personal errands to run.

Your dutiful disciple,

Zhi Lan

It was vague and may rouse suspicion, but Master Dan never pried. She hoped he wouldn't think she had abandoned him. When she came back with the painting, it would all be made clear to him.

Zhi Lan glanced across the room where the thief was still sleeping. If she were to walk out of this room with him, he would need a disguise, and fast. She considered stealing one of Master Dan's ensembles, but it would be hard to explain why she was suddenly in the company of an unnamed scholar if she were caught in the manor. She had better find him some servants' clothes.

The servants' quarters were located further back in the west wing, and after convincing a maid that she was looking for a spare blanket, Zhi Lan managed to grab one of the servants' uniforms from the shelves. She only hoped it would fit.

She hurried back into her room, making sure to close the door swiftly behind her. She was relieved to see the thief still there, but her relief quickly turned into indignation.

He was sitting at the desk where she had written Master Dan's note. Except the desk was now covered in the contents of her bag. Her brushes, pigments, scrap pieces of silk, and the practice books Master Dan had given her demonstrating the standard subjects and techniques of a mountain and river painter, were splayed out as if on a market display. The thief didn't even have the face to look ashamed.

"Just so you know, I have nothing good to steal," Zhi Lan said, irritated.

"I wasn't going to steal anything." He picked up a piece of silk from the pile. It had a half-finished painting of a sparrow on it. "What's this?"

Zhi Lan snatched it back. "None of your business."

They were scraps of primed silk from Master Dan, only about a hand's width wide. Zhi Lan had used them to practice. Some turned out nice enough to make into fans, though she never had the courage to solicit a fan maker to mount and sell them for her. She had a feeling she wouldn't be taken seriously. It was a business venture for later, when she and Master Dan had garnered more fame.

"If you're this stingy with your work, how do you expect to make any money?"

"I don't! Because petty thieves like you might rob me blind," she shot back. She shoved the servant's clothes at him. "Hurry and change. The house will be awake soon."

He looked down at the clothing. "You condemn stealing, yet these are stolen."

Zhi Lan sputtered. "I-I'll return them eventually."

"How so? Will you have me strip in the road when you're done with me?"

She resisted the urge to scream. This was utter madness. She was exhausted, but her heart and mind were racing. She didn't want to think too hard about what she was going to do.

Zhi Lan directed him behind the screen. "*Hurry*. We should go before anyone else wakes up."

"We?"

"I'm coming with you."

There was a beat of silence behind the screen. "If it pleases you."

None of this pleased her, but Zhi Lan didn't waste her breath to argue. She quickly splashed her face with yesterday's water and twisted her hair up with her pins. Then, she repacked her bag and looped her money pouch at her belt. Zhi Lan looked down at her current outfit—a simple bodice, a hemp outer robe, and an old skirt with wrinkled pleats. It would have to do. She doubted she needed to look all that presentable traipsing into a criminal lair. Or a demon's lair.

"I ought to know your name, if we're going to travel together," she said, unnerved by the silence broken only by the soft swish of fabric.

The rustling from behind the screen paused. "It's Shao Qing."

It was a surprisingly boyish name, reminiscent of youth and springtide greens. It didn't suit him at all.

"No family name?" Zhi Lan asked.

"I have no family."

Not surprising. Zhi Lan wrung her hands together. She figured she should get one thing straight before stepping outside with him. And there was no polite way to say it.

"And what are you?"

Another pause. "I don't understand what you mean."

Zhi Lan pressed her hand to her cheek. Who knew

questioning a criminal could be so mortifying? "Your eyes. They're..."

Her words trailed off when Shao Qing emerged.

He had removed his scarf, revealing a straight nose, full lips, and a well-defined jaw. The steel blue servant's uniform he donned was simple, but in much better condition than his previous dirty robes, the neatly pressed lines complimenting his broad shoulders and narrow hips.

The stinky vagabond was handsome.

"Rest assured, Miss Nong. I am as human as they come," Shao Qing said.

Zhi Lan nodded woodenly. Somehow she was even more convinced now that he was a demon. It didn't make sense for a criminal to have such beautiful features.

She couldn't help the blush that rose to her cheeks, which irritated her. She refused to lose her head just because he had an uncommonly handsome face.

"Let's go then," Zhi Lan said.

Shao Qing inclined his head.

THEY BARELY MADE IT FIVE paces across the courtyard before they were seen.

Lady Bu stepped out of the main hall, accompanied by a maid. The lady's eyes locked on hers. There was no escaping the meeting now.

"Lady Bu! Good morning." Zhi Lan clasped her hands and bowed.

A waft of jasmine perfume washed over her as Lady Bu approached. "You're the student of Master Dan, yes? We didn't have the pleasure of speaking yesterday. What is your name again?"

"Nong Zhi Lan, your ladyship."

She stole a look at Lady Bu. Up close, the magistrate's wife was even more beautiful. She wore several layers of light silk robes, all varying shades of purple. Her hair was done up exquisitely, held together by golden pins, complementing her swan-like neck. Zhi Lan figured this was the closest she'd get to a noblewoman in her lifetime.

"Zhi Lan. Like an orchid," Lady Bu said softly, folding her pale hands in front of her. "You do have the looks of a flower in bloom."

Zhi Lan blushed. "Thank you, your ladyship." A compliment from a woman was infinitely more flattering than one from a man.

"Are you finding your stay here comfortable?"

Not in the slightest. "Yes, of course."

Lady Bu smiled. "I must apologize for my husband's behavior the other night. His temper is...unpleasant at times."

"Magistrate Bu's anger was understandable," Zhi Lan said quickly. She heard Shao Qing scoff under his breath, and she scrambled to conceal the sound by coughing loudly into her sleeve. "Excuse me."

Lady Bu smiled. The expression became her, and Zhi Lan realized she hadn't seen her smile at all in the magistrate's presence. "Are you going somewhere?" the lady asked.

"Yes! I have errands to run for my master."

"One typically doesn't leave the ward without a pass."

"Oh. I-I didn't know." Zhi Lan bemoaned her fate for a minute before Lady Bu produced an intricately carved wooden badge from her belt and presented it to her.

"You may show this to the guards on your way out," she said. "It's my personal pass."

Zhi Lan took the pass with both hands. "Thank you, your ladyship!"

"You will be back today, yes?"

Zhi Lan glanced behind her at Shao Qing, who was standing quietly with downcast eyes. He didn't seem to notice her silent question, so she turned back. "I hope so, your ladyship," she said, hazarding a guess.

Lady Bu's gaze slid curiously to Shao Qing. "This is…?"

"One of your manor's servants," Zhi Lan blurted out. "I'm borrowing him for the day, if that's alright. To carry the cargo."

The lady studied him for a moment. Zhi Lan hoped she didn't immediately know that Shao Qing was not part of her staff. Ma claimed rich folks never remembered their servants' faces.

To Zhi Lan's relief, that seemed to be true. Lady Bu stepped aside and gestured to the gate.

"I'll not keep you, then," she said.

Zhi Lan bowed again. "Thank you for your generosity, Lady Bu."

They made it past the manor gate without so much as a nod from the guards. Zhi Lan breathed a sigh of relief as she and Shao Qing headed down the street. She looked back at the front gates of Magistrate Bu's manor. Bold calligraphy was pasted on the doors, reading "Fortune and Virtue". She had found very little of either within those walls.

It was still relatively quiet outside. Zhi Lan inhaled and turned to the thief. "Where did you stash Master Dan's painting?" she whispered. "Somewhere dry, I hope."

"I don't have it."

The sky seemed to crash down on her in that moment. Zhi Lan wobbled on her feet. "What?"

Shao Qing spared her a sideways glance. "I don't know where the painting is."

"Then did you sell it? So quickly?" Zhi Lan demanded. She had expected a quick errand. This was unprecedented.

"My superior has it. Perhaps he already sold it, perhaps not."

"Your superior?"

He nodded.

Shao Qing was in a band of thieves! It was bad enough she had to deal with one. Now she had to face a criminal *leader*. This was exactly the sort of trouble Ma had thought she would get into in the city.

"Then we better hurry," Zhi Lan said, hoping her voice didn't waver. She'd much rather be paint shopping instead of following a stranger into a den of criminals. But this was all for Master Dan and to ensure that both of them would be able to secure their fortune—and make it out alive. "Where does your superior live?"

"I can't share that information," Shao Qing said. "It would be better if I went alone."

Zhi Lan clenched her jaw. "I won't tell anyone."

"I can't take your word for that."

"I'm going even if it means you have to blindfold me!"

He seemed to properly consider this. Zhi Lan wanted to kick herself. She had quite literally volunteered herself to be kidnapped!

"There's no need," Shao Qing finally said. "If Yao catches any constables in his vicinity, he'll take care of you himself."

Zhi Lan recoiled at that. "Well...fine!" Couldn't be worse than hanging in the gallows. "Lead the way."

"As you wish."

He headed down toward the ward gate that led to the rest of the city. Zhi Lan's heart beat wildly in her chest as she showed the guards Lady Bu's pass. She was half convinced they were going to take one look at Shao Qing and pronounce him a thief, but the guards merely gave the pass a cursory glance before letting them through. She nearly melted with relief and tucked the badge into her sleeve.

Zhi Lan was only vaguely familiar with Zhu City's marketplace and the vicinity around Magistrate Bu's manor. She and Master Dan had only been in the city for a week before Magistrate Bu discovered them. Shao Qing, however, seemed to know every nook and cranny like the back of his hand. He took strange paths, ducking through corner shops and weaving into shadowy alleyways. Zhi Lan clutched her bag to her chest and hurried after him, feeling somewhat like a criminal herself.

They came to the end of an alleyway blocked off by a door nailed shut by a cracked wooden board. Shao Qing found an invisible foothold on the surface and climbed up like a cat, jumping onto the other side.

"Why are we traveling like we're guilty?" Zhi Lan panted, climbing onto a rickety pile of crates and barrels.

"You're still here," Shao Qing said from the other side. His head appeared from over the door as he straightened.

"Of course I'm still here!" Zhi Lan cried. "We agreed you would take me to Master Dan's painting, or have you already forgotten that?"

Or he was deliberately trying to lose her. The scoundrel.

"Why does it matter so much? Let your master paint another one," he said.

Zhi Lan lifted her skirts and stepped onto another crate, holding out her hand for balance. "He can't just paint another one!" She knew her master well enough. Last night he hadn't even attempted to lift his brush, as if he had already given up. "The magistrate explicitly said he wants an exact replica."

"I don't see how that's not possible."

"It can't be replicated! Master Dan painted Shui Jin Mountain on site. The brushstrokes, the composition, it was all spontaneous! It came at a moment of inspiration."

Zhi Lan wobbled, the crates creaking in protest. A firm hand grasped hers. Shao Qing guided her to the top most barrel—which reeked of vomit and alcohol—and Zhi Lan managed to step over and straddle the door. The floor on the other side was thankfully more elevated. She stumbled down. Unfortunately, she stumbled right into Shao Qing's arms.

"It is only lines and ink, is it not?" he said, glancing down at her. "You copy the paintings and techniques of other artists. Why is it impossible to copy your own?"

Zhi Lan tried not to notice the sturdiness of his chest or shoulders. "There is a freshness to a spontaneous mark. It cannot be replicated. The result would be utterly soulless."

He smiled at that, an odd sort of smile that didn't reach his eyes. Zhi Lan shuddered. *Nothing* seemed to reach his eyes. She quickly extricated herself and brushed off her robes, wondering if he had deliberately held her for that long to nettle her.

"I doubt the magistrate will be able to tell the difference," Shao Qing said. "He only wants it for the sake of his pride."

Zhi Lan set her jaw. "Even so—"

A small street urchin scampered up to her, no older than seven or eight.

"Miss, mister? Might you spare some change?"

The girl's dirt-streaked face was thin, framed by matted hair. She looked like she hadn't washed or eaten for ages.

Zhi Lan's heart melted a little for the poor child. She reached for the money pouch at her belt—but her hands met air. It was gone.

"We don't have any money. Be on your way," Shao Qing said.

"But—"

"On your way," he repeated, clamping a hand over the urchin's shoulder and pushing her aside. There was a faint clinking sound.

The urchin squeaked and scampered away.

Zhi Lan frowned. "That wasn't very nice."

"Neither were they." Shao Qing jutted his chin to the two small figures that disappeared around the corner. One of them was the girl urchin, the other was a boy Zhi Lan hadn't seen.

Shao Qing held something out to her. She gasped.

"My pouch!" She snatched it back from him. "You stole it!"

"They would've stolen it if I hadn't first. I recommend you keep your belongings somewhere more intimate."

Zhi Lan's eye twitched. She stuffed the pouch into her left sleeve.

They seemed to have passed through to the more impoverished side of the city, where the buildings weren't quite so grand and the streets more unevenly paved. Zhi Lan knew there was a more direct path to the outskirts of the city—across the large bridge. He *had* been trying to lose her!

"I won't give up so easily, so don't bother trying that again." Zhi Lan meant this as a threat, but really she was tired of jumping over walls.

Shao Qing glanced over his shoulder. "Trying what?"

She scowled, narrowing her eyes at him. This thief was as slippery as a river fish.

They walked for some time, Shao Qing always a few steps ahead with his longer strides. Thankfully he took a more straightforward path this time on the main roads. They passed by market stalls and a public bath house. Zhi Lan's stomach growled. She hadn't eaten since last night's banquet, and she was already exhausted, but she carried on, determined to follow this errand to the end. After she got Master Dan's painting, she'd eat as much as she liked.

The streets slowly populated as the sun rose higher in the sky. It seemed to Zhi Lan that they had walked for ages before the buildings grew more sparse, and straw cottages peppered the landscape in the distance, framed by the sprightly greens of the bamboo forest. The scene was beautiful and quaint, reminding her of her quiet village. She wished she had the leisure to paint it.

In her admiration, she hadn't realized Shao Qing had stopped abruptly. Zhi Lan stumbled into his back, then righted herself.

"Have we arrived?" Zhi Lan looked around in confusion. They were still in the market, but they had stopped on the street between a tea house and an herbalist's shop. Did the criminal leader live here?

She glanced down.

A small red pouch had fallen from somewhere on Shao Qing's person. It had a blue silken tassel and a peach embroidered on the front. A rather feminine ornament for a man.

She bent to pick it up. The pouch was soft and well worn at the edges, though it appeared to be empty. "You dropped this."

Shao Qing turned, looking somewhat disoriented before his eyes focused on the trinket pouch. A crease appeared between his brows and he swiftly took it from her, tucking it into the front folds of his robe. An intimate keepsake, then. Was it from a lover?

Zhi Lan didn't have time to wonder.

"Forward," Shao Qing said curtly. He continued on at a brisker pace than before.

PART II
TO KNOW A THIEF

6

SHAO QING HAD AVOIDED TAKING the direct path to Yao's house for years. But Miss Nong had been out of breath and pink in the face just from climbing over a few crates. He figured she would not appreciate his usual wayward route, so he had obliged her.

He brought his hand to his brow, shielding his eyes from the sun as the paved street turned into a dirt road. Reminiscing produced a sour discomfort in his stomach. Those street urchins had reminded him too much of himself, and he hadn't seen the herbalist shop in years. The proprietor, Master Cai, had been the first businessman to offer Shao Qing a job and the first to treat him with kindness. Shao Qing wondered if he still worked there.

His discomfort faded into his usual passivity the closer they came to their destination. A glance behind his shoulder showed Miss Nong several paces behind, half walking and half trotting to catch up with him.

At the end of the dirt path sat Yao's house. It was a modest cottage, the roof thatched with fresh straw, surrounded by trees and sparse stalks of bamboo. A fence enclosed a garden and a few chickens, which squawked when Shao Qing approached. Beside them was the sturdy figure of Yao's wife. An Qin had a basket tucked under one tanned arm, her sleeves hiked to her elbows as she scattered handfuls of chicken feed.

"Shao Qing? We weren't expecting you today," An Qin called out.

He bowed. "I'm here to see Yao."

Miss Nong finally caught up to him, panting. She tossed her hair behind her shoulder. There were wisps coming out from her pins and sticking to her temples.

"My, who's this?" An Qin said, raising her brows. "A lady friend of yours?"

"An acquaintance," Miss Nong bit out. The breach of politeness was only temporary. She quickly clasped her hands and bowed. "I'm Nong Zhi Lan, madam."

An Qin pushed open the fence, a smile spreading over her face. "A pleasure, Miss Nong."

"Oh, I'm no treasured miss. Please call me Zhi Lan."

Shao Qing wondered if that also applied to him. Miss Nong *was* overly formal. Her given name suited her more. He found himself absently studying the curve of her neck. It did have the elegant arch of an orchid plant.

"Zhi Lan, then. I'm An Qin."

"You have a lovely home, madam," Zhi Lan said, turning her gaze to the cottage roof. "It's crowned in bamboo."

A dimple appeared on An Qin's face. "You're a sweet one. I reckon you're here to see Yao too? I hope he didn't rob you blind or anything of the sort."

"Is Yao home?" Shao Qing cut in.

An Qin waved her hand. "He is, but not fit for guests. He's terribly hungover."

Zhi Lan threw a desperate glance his way.

"We'd like to see him now," Shao Qing said.

An Qin raised a brow. "I suppose the children are already bothering him anyway. Come with me." She ducked inside the cottage through a low wooden door frame.

Shao Qing began to follow, but Zhi Lan tugged his sleeve. "Are you sure this is the right place?" she whispered. "This seems awfully...domestic."

She had taken to walking close behind him, as if she expected danger to spring out at any moment and he were her shield. Shao Qing extricated his sleeve. "This is the place. There's no need to be afraid."

Zhi Lan straightened her hunched shoulders and raised her chin. "Who said I was afraid?"

"Your body. Stop cowering."

She harrumphed and pushed past him. Getting a reaction out of her was oddly satisfying, like throwing a stone into a still pond.

Inside, Yao's two children ran to and fro, squealing boisterously. They were about four or five, too young to pay the newcomers any mind, and continued to wreak havoc around the wooden table behind which Yao himself sat with his fingers pressed to his temples.

"Elder Brother Yao," Shao Qing said to announce himself.

Yao squinted up at him. "Brother Qing? What are you doing here?" He scowled. "Don't tell me someone got caught last night."

"Not that I know of."

"I'm turning you in myself if any of us gets implicated."

Shao Qing shrugged. "I'm here about the painting."

"If it's about the profits, everyone gets an equal cut. Just because you barreled in recklessly doesn't mean—" Yao stopped abruptly when he caught sight of Zhi Lan. His eyebrows shot to his hairline. "What's this? Have you found yourself a woman?"

An Qin slid into the seat beside him. "That's what I said! Who knew Shao Qing had it in him to attract such a pretty girl?"

Zhi Lan shot Shao Qing an accusing glare when he didn't correct them. She turned to Yao and executed another bow. "I'm Nong Zhi Lan, sir. You must be Shao Qing's superior."

Yao barked an explosive laugh. "She's wearing white! Is she mourning? Or is she a scholar?"

"She's a painter's apprentice," Shao Qing said.

"Indeed?" Yao said. "What does she want from you?"

"She's right here," Zhi Lan said irritably, seeming to have gotten over her initial fright.

"Don't mind the stupid men," An Qin said in a consoling tone. "Have you eaten yet?"

An answering growl came from Zhi Lan's stomach.

An Qin ushered the children away and made Shao Qing and Zhi Lan sit with Yao at the table. In five minutes she set a steaming bowl of noodle soup before each of them.

Shao Qing picked up his chopsticks and began to eat. He never felt particularly hungry, but he knew his body needed the fuel.

Zhi Lan looked hesitantly into her bowl.

"We're not going to poison you, if that's what you're afraid of," An Qin said.

"Oh no! I didn't mean...it looks delicious." Zhi Lan dipped her spoon into the broth and gingerly took a sip.

Yao leaned back into his chair, his gaze narrowed on her. "So, what is it you want from me, young miss?"

Zhi Lan shot Shao Qing a hesitant look. He nodded at her. It was her story to tell, and Shao Qing certainly didn't feel like speaking for her on top of everything else.

"Well...I'm not sure if you know this, sir, but my master and I are under the patronage of Magistrate Bu."

"You work for the magistrate?"

Zhi Lan squirmed under Yao's gaze. "Well, n-not really. The thing is, his lordship is upset about the painting that you—er, that *was* stolen yesterday. He wanted it for his collection. The disappearance is...affecting us negatively. I was wondering if...if I could possibly get it back?"

Yao stared for a moment before exploding into another hearty laugh. Shao Qing was impressed he wasn't giving himself a headache.

"This girl is either extremely bold or extremely naive. And naive isn't your type, is it, Brother Qing?" Yao nudged Shao Qing's shoulder.

"Please stop speaking of me as if I'm not in the room," Zhi Lan said with a frown. "And for the record, I am *not* romantically involved with him."

Yao grinned at this. It seemed he decided she wasn't a threat after all.

"Really, Yao, stop tormenting the girl." An Qin seated herself beside Zhi Lan. "What's this about? Was it that painting you sent off last night?"

Zhi Lan set down her spoon. "Sent off?"

"There were multiple I sent off last night," Yao said with a wave of his hand. "Not sure which one you're talking about, young miss."

A pink flush colored Zhi Lan's cheeks when she turned to Shao Qing. "Shao Qing, tell him!"

He took a sip of soup. "The one with the mountain and all the plants."

Yao tsked. "You're going to have to be more specific than that."

Zhi Lan looked ready to explode.

"Perhaps you could sketch it for us?" Yao suggested.

"I don't think there's time," she said curtly.

Yao shrugged a shoulder. "Can't help you if I don't know what painting you're talking about."

Zhi Lan inhaled slowly, seeming to steel herself. "Paper and brush, if you please."

An Qin brought out a sheet of paper, an old inkstone and inkstick, and a frayed brush that had seen better days. Zhi

Lan wrinkled her nose delicately as she picked up the ink-stick, worn to little more than a nub, and began grinding it into the inkstone with a few drops of water.

Her motions were elegant, from the way she held her sleeve to the way she poised the brush over the paper, as if she were a well-bred lady instead of a farm girl. She sketched in confident strokes. First, the outline of the silk scroll on which the painting was mounted, then the painting itself—a composition of mountains and waterfalls and flora in the foreground.

Shao Qing found her movements fascinating, as well as the serene concentration on her face as she executed them. He didn't realize he was staring until Yao kicked him under the table and waggled his eyebrows. Shao Qing returned his attention to his noodles.

"Here," Zhi Lan said, setting down her brush and turning the paper to Yao. "It's only an approximation of my master's but you recognize it, I hope?"

Yao took the sketch. "Ah, yes! The fresh-as-an-orange-peel painting."

Zhi Lan furrowed her brows. "It's a waterfall, not an orange peel."

"No, it is fresh, like an orange peel," Yao said. "This is very good too."

"Oh. Um. Thank you," Zhi Lan said. "So...where is the original?"

"I sold it already," Yao said. "To Magistrate Li in the next city."

Zhi Lan wrung her hands together. "You sold it to a magistrate? If I explain my situation to him, will he give it back?"

An Qin slapped her knee. "Oh, that is rich! He would never relinquish it if he knew it's Magistrate Bu's."

"Why not?" Zhi Lan asked.

"Ah, this you don't know," An Qin said. "Magistrate Bu and Magistrate Li have a public feud, you see. The two magistrates were academic rivals back in their scholar days, always attempting to outdo each other."

"I don't see how this pertains to the issue."

An Qin leaned forward eagerly, as if she had been waiting for ages to relay this piece of gossip to new ears. Shao Qing himself had heard the story too many times to count. "The current Lady Bu is Magistrate Li's eldest daughter."

Zhi Lan nodded, still looking confused.

"She is his favorite child. Magistrate Li originally wanted a more advantageous marriage for her, but he was bound by a promise his father made to betroth Lady Bu to Magistrate Bu. The late Master Li liked Magistrate Bu. But the current Magistrate Li did everything he could to subvert the marriage. It was all for naught, however, and only worsened their rivalry."

Zhi Lan blinked. "I see."

An Qin tsked. "It was said after the marriage had taken place, Lady Bu sent a letter home saying how she hated living in Zhu City, and how Magistrate Bu wasn't kind to her. But the letter ended up in the hands of a gossipmonger and soon everyone in both cities knew. Magistrate Bu was incensed when word got back to him—quite shameful to have one's dirty laundry aired out. So he made it a point to make his manor identical to Magistrate Li's, if only to put on a show that he dotes on his wife. He had all the carpenters in the city occupied for months. He heard Magistrate Li was a great admirer of art, so Magistrate Bu began his collection too."

"I was under the impression Magistrate Bu began his art collection in his student days," Zhi Lan said, looking surprised.

"Pah. That's only what he claims. He acquired his taste for art only to outdo Magistrate Li."

"But that's so childish!" Zhi Lan exclaimed. She seemed drawn into the story now, her eyes widening ever so slightly.

"Exactly!" An Qin crowed. "There's nothing better than grown men engaging in petty disagreements. It is food for the soul, I tell you."

Zhi Lan laughed, the sound bright, like a silver bell.

"There is, however, a rumor," An Qin said, dropping her voice to a whisper. "They say Magistrate Bu crossed the line."

Zhi Lan leaned forward. "How so?"

"Twenty years ago Magistrate Li's eldest son had produced a child. His first grandchild! But on the night of its birth, the baby disappeared."

Zhi Lan gasped. "You don't mean to say Magistrate Bu kidnapped Magistrate Li's grandchild!"

"If it's true, it's indeed terrible," An Qin said solemnly. "But Magistrate Li's family never confirmed or denied. It's a rather embarrassing thing, for such crimes to fall upon a magistrate's family and go unsolved. Perhaps it is only a wild rumor."

Zhi Lan frowned, her lower lip sticking out in a slight pout. Yao nudged Shao Qing's arm. "Stare any longer and you'll wear a hole through her head," he said in a low voice. Then in a louder voice before Shao Qing could respond, he said, "So you see, young miss, Magistrate Li will never willingly give up an item he procured from Magistrate Bu."

Zhi Lan furrowed her brow. "But...why would a magistrate want stolen goods?"

"Injustice runs rampant even in those who enforce justice, young miss," Yao said. "I myself supply Magistrate Li's stolen art. He's a willing buyer. But if *you* want to steal it back, you're welcome to do so."

"Who said anything about stealing?" she asked in a bewildered tone. "The painting *belongs* to my master. I only want it back. You can help us, can't you, sir?"

"Stealing is the only way you're going to get it back," Yao said firmly. "I certainly won't offend my wealthiest client by retracting a sale."

Zhi Lan bit her lip, her eyes darting from Yao to Shao Qing to the sketch on the table.

Shao Qing was convinced she was going to burst into tears. But to his surprise, Zhi Lan asked, "Where does Magistrate Li live?"

A slow smile spread across Yao's face. An Qin threw up her hands.

"Oh, look at you, corrupting an innocent girl," she said. "I can hardly sit back and watch."

"You should've thought of that before we married, my treasure," Yao said.

An Qin threw up her hands again. "I'll be in the kitchen!" She cleared off the bowls on the table and went past a rough-spun curtain to the adjoining room.

Yao turned back to Zhi Lan. "I will help, young miss."

Shao Qing raised an eyebrow. "You'll help?"

"I'd like to see you get out of this scrape. I'll be waiting for a good story by the end of it," Yao whispered to him. "If you survive."

Shao Qing figured the thief lord must be in one of his playful moods. He was always in better spirits sober than drunk.

Then, Yao turned to Zhi Lan. "Magistrate Li is in Yun City. You'll have to head east to the intercity gates. It's unlikely you'll make it before curfew today. The gates close at dusk. Do you have your papers?"

Zhi Lan made a noise. "I left them behind."

"Not a problem. A thief should never cross city gates with genuine papers. We'll forge them," Yao said.

She looked slightly ill at this.

"Once you make it to Yun City, you'll be able to find your way to Magistrate Li's manor easily enough. The homes of the wealthy are not difficult to spot and every civilian knows where the magistrate is located. As for the stealing part...well, let Shao Qing handle that. He finds sadistic joy in last-minute heists."

Yao then drew up a crude layout of Magistrate Li's manor. It was similar to many of the aristocratic courtyard houses, with one main wing, an east and west wing, and the front gates.

"There's a pond behind the main wing that connects to a river. You can make your escape that way, if things become dire."

Shao Qing had never been on a heist that took him to Yun City, even though it was right next door. According to Yao, Magistrate Li ran a tighter ship than Magistrate Bu did. Yun City's guards were always suspicious and Shao Qing's light eyes made him too recognizable. But the prospect of going somewhere new was enticing. And he wanted to see Zhi Lan squirm at the idea of becoming a thief, if only to entertain himself.

"Give me an hour to forge your papers," Yao said. "An Qin will prepare some food for the road."

Zhi Lan stood and bowed. "Thank you for your help. I...wasn't expecting generosity when I came here," she admitted.

Yao waved his hand. "Well, a friend of Shao Qing is a friend of mine. He *did* save my life. The least I can do is assist him from time to time."

A pretty lie for Zhi Lan. Shao Qing was sure the only reason Yao was doing this was because he was starved of entertainment, though he was surprised by the amount of effort the thief lord was willing to put in to attain it.

Shao Qing saw Zhi Lan shoot him a bewildered look at his periphery. "You saved his life?"

"If that's what you want to call it," he said.

Shao Qing had first come across Yao three years ago, lying unconscious in a muddy ditch. He had dragged him up to see if the older man had anything worth stealing in his pockets, but Yao had woken up and punched him in the face.

"So you see, if he hadn't pulled me out to steal from me, I would've been eaten by a leash of foxes. The animals were running rampant that time of year. Quite feral. My body would've been unrecognizable," Yao said.

"Ah. How...fortunate," Zhi Lan said faintly.

Although Shao Qing hadn't meant to do it, saving Yao's life turned out to be beneficial. He had been stealing on his own before then, but only petty street thefts for mere survival—nothing on a grand scale.

Once he joined Yao's gang, Shao Qing never went a day without a roof over his head and food in his belly. They stole silk scrolls and prized vases and bronze sculptures from manors of the wealthy. The thrill of each heist stole the air from his lungs and brought vibrant color to the corners of his vision.

But lately, this lifestyle had grown too routine, the excitement long since dulled.

Shao Qing wondered if this excursion could rekindle that excitement.

7

AFTER YAO HAD FINISHED FORGING their papers, An Qin saw the two of them off with a bundle of steamed buns.

The city was fully awake now, the streets crowded in the late afternoon. Much to her embarrassment, Zhi Lan had to grab the back of Shao Qing's belt so she wouldn't lose him.

Her feet grew sore after they had walked a little over halfway through the city. Luckily, they came across a generous merchant who allowed them to ride on the back of his cart in exchange for some of An Qin's steamed buns. Zhi Lan and Shao Qing ate the rest. The buns were still warm, stuffed with cabbage and pork, and Zhi Lan savored every bite. But when dusk began to paint the horizon with its hazy purples and pinks, she grew hungry again.

"We'll have to stop for today," Shao Qing said.

The merchant dropped them off before a tea house in a busy street, as his path diverged with theirs. Zhi Lan watched the cart disappear regretfully.

"Are you sure we can't make it to the gate?" Zhi Lan stood on her tiptoes in an attempt to see the city gate, though to no avail. Her view was blocked by tall buildings with upturned eaves, lit by red and yellow lanterns.

"It's still miles away," Shao Qing said. "We'll get there in the morning."

Zhi Lan sighed, wishing they had a horse drawn carriage like the wealthy folk. A journey between the neighboring cities would take half a day at most. "I hate leaving Master Dan at a time like this. He must be worried."

With some unease, she recalled that the magistrate had given them three days to complete a duplicate painting. The first day was coming to a close. She didn't know if a magistrate could hang anyone he pleased—there *were* laws, after all. But he was a powerful man. He was meant to enforce the law. Perhaps he could bend it too.

There was no use thinking such grim thoughts now. The faster Zhi Lan completed this errand, the faster she'd be able to give Master Dan good news.

Shao Qing tilted his head to the tea house, not bothering to appease or comfort her. Not that she expected it.

"Let's go, then," Zhi Lan said with a sigh.

The tea house had two levels and was bustling with city folk taking their evening meals. A server scampered up and guided them to a table on the upper level where they had a bird's-eye view of the ground floor through an intricately carved wooden railing. They were served tea, and Zhi Lan picked out a few dishes after Shao Qing made no move to do so.

Her attention wandered as they waited for their food. On the level below, a small stage graced the center, where an elderly man was telling a dramatized tale to an enraptured audience, gesturing with his white fan.

Zhi Lan perked up when she recognized the story. It was about a snake spirit who had become human to repay her benefactor, a young man studying medicine. The two end up falling in love and marrying, despite the meddling of a self-righteous abbot.

"The Legend of the White Snake!" Zhi Lan said, delighted. It was her favorite story, one that she begged Ma to tell her over and over again when she was little. "It's so romantic, isn't it?"

Shao Qing took a sip of his tea. "It's impossible for a demon to have feelings. They are heartless creatures."

Zhi Lan arched a brow. "How would you know? People have the capacity to be heartless. There could very well be demons who possess humanity."

"It's impossible," Shao Qing said.

"I disagree."

He inclined his head and went back to his tea.

"For a stubborn man you're not very argumentative," Zhi Lan said.

"Why argue when we've each made our stances clear?"

Zhi Lan was determined to get a reaction out of him, if only to pass the time.

"Even if it is impossible," she said, "that is what makes the story so compelling. Surely *your* favorite story has impossibilities."

"I don't have a favorite story."

As she processed that bland reply, the server came back with food. There was half a steamed fish, two bowls of rice, and a selection of pickled vegetables. Zhi Lan thanked him, bringing a slice of lotus root to her mouth with her chopsticks. It was braised in a flavorful sweet and savory sauce, the texture delightfully crisp. The fish was tender and perfectly seasoned with ginger and salt. The slices of pickled radish on the side were tart and refreshing. Zhi Lan sighed in satisfaction with each new flavor. Meals on the farm had always been plain—they never had such a variety of spices in their pantries. City food had certainly spoiled her.

When the dishes were done, the server stopped by with a platter of peaches. Zhi Lan took one eagerly, peeling the soft pink skin away to reveal white flesh. There was nothing better than a perfectly ripened summer peach.

She was halfway done with the fruit when she realized Shao Qing was staring at her.

Zhi Lan wiped her mouth self-consciously. "What?"

"You're like a little girl," Shao Qing said with a slow blink.

"How so?"

"You look as if that peach is the best thing that has ever happened to you."

Zhi Lan finished her peach, setting the pit and the skin neatly into her empty rice bowl. "So what, just because I'm grown I can't enjoy things?" she challenged. When Shao Qing made no reply, she grumbled under her breath, "What do you know of children anyway?" She was annoyed he kept comparing her to one.

Shao Qing was staring at nothing in the distance, seemingly not up for conversation.

She frowned. Zhi Lan still couldn't quite figure him out. He refused to give those street urchins money, which marked him as an ungenerous person. Yet he had saved Yao's life and he was helping her without demanding anything in return. She had threatened him, of course. But halfway through the day as they were walking through crowds, Shao Qing had waited patiently for her to catch up to him. Zhi Lan knew a thief could easily escape from a lone girl unfamiliar with the city.

If she had to describe Shao Qing in a word, it would be impassive. Heartless without being malicious, as if he wasn't entirely aware of himself. It was very strange. Perhaps he was only excessively bland because he had a handsome face. There was no need for a handsome man to have a pleasant personality. Or he had taken a monk's vow and sworn off everything worldly and pleasurable, including good conversation.

Zhi Lan shook her head, turning her attention to stacking the empty dishes. She was only here to get Master Dan's painting back. It hardly mattered whether her guide was a monk, a thief, or simply boring. All he needed to be was true to his word.

So far, he had been.

Night fell quickly and soon the crowd in the tea house dispersed, some retreating to their rented rooms, others finding lodging elsewhere. Zhi Lan opened her money pouch. She had brought a full string of coins with her, but somehow they had all come loose, the knotted cord holding them together untied. Her bag felt lighter too. She narrowed her eyes at Shao Qing, who was a small figure downstairs. He had gone to inquire about available rooms in the tea house. Zhi Lan placed a few coins on their table and went down to join him.

"How many rooms do you require, sir?" the owner, a short man with a sparse mustache, asked. "Any preference for size?"

"One. The cheapest you have." Shao Qing kept his eyes lowered, perhaps to hide their strange color. Zhi Lan felt a pang of pity for him, wondering if he'd been ostracized for it. But the thought quickly dissipated when she realized what he just said.

The owner raised a derisive eyebrow.

"One?" Zhi Lan hissed under her breath.

Shao Qing glanced over at her. "Do you have money to pay for two?"

"*I'm* paying?"

"Seeing as I'm not, yes," Shao Qing said.

The tea house owner watched this exchange with obvious bewilderment. "Miss, who is this man to you?" he asked.

"Er...he's my—"

"Husband," Shao Qing said.

"Right," Zhi Lan said weakly.

The owner shot him a dirty look. "You make your wife pay your expenses? Do you even deserve to call yourself a man?"

"I asked for a room, not a lecture," Shao Qing said.

The owner shook his head disbelievingly. "Very well, follow me."

He led them down a back hallway that was dark and cluttered with miscellaneous items. Zhi Lan passed the large, decorative head of a lion costume, wondering if a traveling performance troupe had left it in haste. They descended a narrow flight of stairs, turned a dark corner, and stopped in front of a sliding door. Mold speckled the wooden frame and there were holes poked into the paper screen as if someone had stuck their finger through it to peek inside. In short, it was the seediest room Zhi Lan ever had the displeasure of paying for.

She handed the owner the money with a clink, though he seemed reluctant to accept the coins. He took his leave with a bow, shooting one last glare at Shao Qing before he disappeared into the shadowy hall.

Zhi Lan peered into her pouch. "We only have two meals left to eat after this so I hope we conclude this business before dinner tomorrow."

"We only have two more *paid* meals," Shao Qing corrected.

She began to reprimand him, but she pressed her lips together. She *was* in the presence of a thief.

Shao Qing slid the door open. It creaked terribly, revealing a small chamber with a shallow alcove bed with white curtains and a rickety table and stool, upon which a melted candle stump sat. It was barely larger than a closet.

"Lovely," Zhi Lan said grouchily.

She hadn't had a good night's sleep last night. Clearly she wouldn't be getting one tonight, either.

Then, with some alarm, she realized she would have to spend the night with Shao Qing. *Again.* The thief in question began to remove his outer robe. After a day of traveling, he smelled even worse, which she didn't think was possible. A mixture of sweat and dirt and man. Zhi Lan pinched her nostrils closed.

There was hardly any floor space to lay down comfortably. And the floorboards were badly stained with mold and some other sticky substance Zhi Lan didn't care to identify. She couldn't make him take the floor with good conscience, but...

Before she could voice her dilemma, Shao Qing sat and stretched his legs over the bed. Zhi Lan looked on awkwardly, clutching her bag to her chest.

They *had* slept in the same room just the other night. But she hadn't been entirely at his mercy, like she was now.

"I won't touch you, if that's what you're worried about," he said.

"I'm not worried," Zhi Lan said quickly.

Shao Qing tipped his head to the inside of the bed.

"Why the inside?" she said suspiciously.

"So I can better protect us if there's an intruder."

Zhi Lan suddenly remembered Shao Qing was a wanted criminal. "Do you think the constables will come after you?" she asked faintly.

"Unlikely. Magistrate Bu is terrible at finding thieves."

This was news to her. "But isn't that his job?"

Shao Qing rearranged the bedding. "If he were good at it, Yao would've long been imprisoned."

Zhi Lan shifted uncomfortably. Magistrate Bu was turning out to be a very different sort of man than she expected. At first, she'd been happy that he had become their patron. Magistrates were supposed to be fair and just—intelligent men with good morals who upheld the same values in the populace. Zhi Lan had been sure that they would be safe and secure under him. Little did she know that Magistrate Bu wasn't very fair, nor apparently was he very intelligent.

"Are you going to sleep standing there?" Shao Qing said.

With a deep breath, Zhi Lan set her things on the table, then awkwardly climbed over Shao Qing's legs into the hard bed, not bothering to remove her outer robe. The more barriers between them, the better.

The sheets smelled like mildew.

Shao Qing laid himself down and closed his eyes. Zhi Lan pushed away her uneasiness as she did the same, making sure to wedge herself into the furthest corner of the alcove. But even then, she was all too aware of the male presence to her left. Skies, what would Ma and Ba think of her, traipsing around with a criminal and sharing a bed with him?

Her desperation to save Master Dan and her future was truly unmatched.

Zhi Lan turned on her side and covered her nose with her sleeve. The unpleasant smells were keeping her from the lull of sleep. She considered confronting Shao Qing about her missing coins. In their current positions, it would be odd pillow talk, but she needed to know—she had intended to send some of her monthly allowance back home, but now there wouldn't be enough. She stole a peek over at him.

Shao Qing's elegant profile was silhouetted in the dim room, his breaths deep and even. Was he asleep already?

Zhi Lan rolled onto her back and crossed her arms. The only time he could've taken the coins was when he'd stolen her pouch. He hadn't touched her at all since he assisted her over the wall, and she was sure he couldn't have managed any slight of hand without making contact. Then the urchins had come and...

Zhi Lan's question died on her lips when she recalled the sound of clinking as Shao Qing had pushed the urchin child away.

And suddenly her opinion of him leaned more favorably.

8

SHAO QING DREAMED AGAIN. IT began the same as all his others. He was a dragon. He was trapped. He was surrounded by darkness.

But suddenly, he was back in the outer wards of Zhu City. The sky was hazy, an evening pink. He was thirteen again, a scrappy errand boy for Master Cai's herbalist shop. A paper parcel in hand, he trotted through the crowded streets of the city, each building and stall familiar. To his left was a stand of spun sugar figures on sticks. To his right, a vendor sold fans and ladies' hairpins.

As he turned into an alleyway, a sense of dread weighed like a pit in his stomach. This moment was ominously familiar. He'd been in the middle of a delivery. He was passing by the alley where he was living with...

Shadows fell over the scene.

No, turn back! he shouted at himself.

But he couldn't. The alleyway grew and warped around him like the dark wings of a bat. There was no escape. Shao

Qing turned his head. A group of rough boys surrounded a scrawny little girl clutching a red silken pouch embroidered with a peach.

Shao Qing grew cold.

The older boy grabbed the girl by the collar, lifting her clean off the ground.

"Hand it over. And tell your brother that all he earns will belong to me, or I'll make both of your lives miserable."

"No!" The little girl kicked and squirmed. She gripped the pouch in her hand, her small, dirt-streaked knuckles turning white.

"What did you say?" the boy demanded.

"I said no! This is our money. Go make your own!"

The boy smirked. "I am." He slammed the girl into the wall.

She cried out and crumpled to the ground, tears welling in her eyes. "M-my brother will g-get you for this," she stammered.

"Will he? Oh, but where is he?" The boy made a show of looking around and his cronies laughed. He kicked her in the ribs. Then again.

Shao Qing stood frozen. His feet were rooted to the ground as the gang of boys beat his little sister like a sack of flour. Like she wasn't a child precious to him.

Su Su, Shao Qing tried to shout, but no sound came out. *I'm coming!*

The red pouch never left Su Su's grasp. She curled her small body around it, protecting it instead of herself because Shao Qing had told her to. Even when she had stopped crying, stopped moving, the boys had to wrestle it from her stiff fingers. They emptied the pouch, laughing as copper coins fell into their awaiting hands.

Shao Qing collapsed to his knees, a wrenching pain in his chest. Then, he was filled with terrible numbness.

His first thought had been to turn back, to protect himself. Not to save his sister. After all this time, he was still a coward.

I'm sorry, Su Su. I'm sorry.

Shudders racked Shao Qing's body. He was dimly aware of wetness streaking his temples. His eyes felt hot and swollen.

"Hush. You'll be alright," came a sleepy murmur. Someone curled against his back and wrapped an arm around his waist. A small hand pressed over the ache in his chest.

Shao Qing inhaled slowly, opening his eyes to darkness. His lashes were wet. He was *crying*. He hadn't cried in six years.

Slowly, his anguish dissipated to a dull ache. Eventually, that dissipated too until there was nothing. He felt like himself again—numb and disoriented.

The faint scent of jasmine soap and pu'er tea curled around him. Shao Qing came to his senses. He was in a room in a tea house with Zhi Lan. It was *her* hand against his chest. *Her* body tucked around his in an intimate, protective way.

It felt…comforting.

WATERY MORNING LIGHT STREAMED IN through the small window, illuminating the dingy beige room. Shao Qing studied the girl on the other side of the pillow.

Zhi Lan was still asleep, far closer than she had been when they went to bed. Her hair was halfway undone, her slender limbs tangled in the sheets. Her delicate features were at rest, not pulled into a face like she was in the habit of doing when awake.

Shao Qing was not unused to the sight of a woman in bed with him. He had spent a night in the arms of a courtesan once, though he heard from the following morning gossip that she found him unsettling.

"Unresponsive, like a boulder," the courtesan had said, and the entire pleasure house had exploded into giggles.

Other men described pleasures of the flesh like reaching a mountain peak—of morning clouds and evening rain. Shao Qing found it awkward at best and messy at worst. It had been a night of overwhelming perfume and a stranger's intimate touch. He had decided that it was not to his taste. It didn't make his blood rush like petty crime did, though he couldn't imagine why.

He and Zhi Lan had no such exchange, yet she had held him like a lover. Nothing in their previous interactions had suggested she desired him in that way. Or he had completely missed the signs.

Slowly, Shao Qing twisted a strand of her ink black hair between his fingers and tugged at it gently.

Zhi Lan's eyes fluttered open.

"Good morning," Shao Qing said.

"What are you *doing*?" she shrieked, sitting up. She patted the front of her clothing, as if making sure they were still there.

Shao Qing stared. An unexpected reaction. "Are you in love with me?"

"Excuse me?" Zhi Lan sputtered. "I barely know you!"

Shao Qing propped himself up on his elbows. "Then you desire my body."

Zhi Lan yanked the pillow from under him and threw it at his head.

He batted it away. "A simple no would suffice."

"Since when do men take no for an answer?" Zhi Lan said darkly, climbing over his legs to reach the edge of the bed.

"Then were you cold?" Shao Qing asked.

"I confess I do not understand this line of questioning." Zhi Lan bent down to pull on her shoes, then she tightened her belt and ran her fingers through her hair. Her pins had fallen off in her excitement, leaving her hair running loose down her back. She patted her head in a panic.

Shao Qing retrieved the two wooden hairpins from the bed and offered them to her. He noticed the tip of one was carved into the shape of an orchid.

Zhi Lan snatched them from his hand and hurriedly twisted up her hair.

"You were holding me last night," Shao Qing said slowly. "Why?"

She stood from the bed and busied herself with tidying the room, straightening her clothes, and rummaging through the things in her bag. "You slept fitfully. I thought you needed comfort," she mumbled, so quickly he barely caught it. There was a flush to her cheeks that hadn't been there before. She went to the basin of water that someone must've delivered when they were both asleep and splashed her face with more violence than necessary.

Shao Qing considered her explanation. He *had* slept fitfully because of his dream. Yet she still had no obligation to comfort him, unless he was disturbing her sleep. He nodded slowly. He must have been bothering her, then.

"This changes nothing, so don't get any ideas," Zhi Lan said after emerging from the basin, her face dripping and pulled into a scowl. She dried herself with a hand towel. "We're going to Yun City today and we're going to get my master's painting. Then you're taking me back immediately. Got it?"

Shao Qing nodded.

"Good." She flung the damp towel at him. "Now get dressed."

9

Thanks to Yao's expertly forged papers, they passed through the city gate with little trouble and entered Yun City. It wasn't so different from Zhu City, with plenty of businesses and market stalls and lively crowds. They even passed by the grand opening of a restaurant that celebrated with long strings of exploding firecrackers. In the adjacent street, there had been a wedding procession. The groom rode at the front in red robes, his bride carried in an ornate red palanquin behind him, surrounded by a procession of lively trumpet players and servants.

Zhi Lan was grateful for the noise, as it made talking nearly impossible. She was still recovering from the mortification of that morning.

She had awoken to Shao Qing laying across from her, playing with her hair like they were lovers, his white inner robe gaping open to expose a smooth sliver of muscled chest. It was a terrifyingly intimate sight, and for a moment her heart had stopped beating.

Then he had the gall to ask if she *desired his body*. Where *did* men find the audacity to say such things?

Zhi Lan felt heat creep to her cheeks at the mere memory. Perhaps she should have just confessed to physical attraction. Somehow that was less embarrassing than the truth. But Shao Qing seemed to have no capacity for embarrassment, so why should she?

Whenever Zhi Lan fell sick, Ma would lay next to her and stroke her back until she fell asleep. It always made her feel better.

Last night, Shao Qing had been shuddering violently. Zhi Lan was worried that he had caught something, but it wasn't until he had spoken that she realized he was crying.

"I'm sorry, Su Su," he had said. There was such pain in his voice.

Zhi Lan had been half asleep herself. Her first instinct had been to comfort him in the only way she knew how. He was clearly a man haunted with terrible regrets, which was more than Zhi Lan had given him credit for. It was quite pitiful. Why else would a careless thief be sorry to the point of tears?

Then it was morning and Shao Qing had gone back to his usual strange self, and Zhi Lan wished she hadn't done anything at all. She had momentarily grown soft toward him and the darkness of night had made her bold. Besides, Zhi Lan was not immune to the appeal of handsome men. It was a difficult situation for any girl to be in. She had merely lost her head in that moment.

"It's early," Shao Qing said, startling her from her thoughts.

"Yes, what about it?" Zhi Lan asked.

After inquiring about directions to Magistrate Li's manor, they finally stood before the abode in question. It was almost identical to Magistrate Bu's. Many of the rich had their court-yard houses laid out and decorated in the same styles. This, however, was on another level. The calligraphy pasted on the doors read "Patience and Virtue" while Magistrate Bu's had read "Fortune and Virtue". Even the color of the roof tiles matched. They really *were* in the middle of some sort of petty bureaucratic feud.

The only difference Zhi Lan could gauge was the greenery bursting from over the manor walls. She spotted the boughs of a willow tree setting loose sprightly green leaves into the wind.

Shao Qing studied the outer gates. "It's not an ideal time to do what we have to do."

"But if we wait until it's dark, it'll take another full day to return," Zhi Lan said impatiently.

Here she was, in an entirely different city while Master Dan was suffering under Magistrate Bu's bad temper all by himself. Zhi Lan itched to get this over with. Soon she'd have the painting in hand, appease Magistrate Bu, and continue to benefit from his patronage and make a name for herself. And she'd never have to associate with criminals again. Especially not stinky, callous, and unbearably handsome ones.

"We don't have to wait until dark," Shao Qing said. "To-day is washing day."

Zhi Lan blinked. She had nearly forgotten, even though her hair was starting to feel unclean.

Every fifth day was washing day. Everyone in office and most civilians took the day off to bathe, either at the public bathhouses, or if one was very rich, in their own homes. In Zhi Lan's village, everyone washed up at the river. There was always a lax energy to the day, as if the entire empire had agreed on a collective vacation.

"You're lucky," Shao Qing said. "Today is the safest day for thieves, even the novices."

Zhi Lan was surprised that someone who clearly didn't bathe remembered what days were washing days. "So...when do *you* bathe?" she ventured to ask.

He glanced at her. "Does it matter?"

"It matters if I have to smell you."

He merely shook his head and continued walking down the street. "We'll wait until it's closer to noon for the changing of the guard. The servants will be busy in the kitchen and the magistrate will likely be bathing."

"What do you propose we do until then?"

"I'll get us a change of clothes."

Zhi Lan looked down at her white robes and Shao Qing's pale blue ones. Both were still clean and intact. "Why?"

"White is too conspicuous."

Shao Qing stuck out a hand, and it wasn't until a second later that Zhi Lan realized he was asking for money. With a long suffering sigh, she dug into her pouch and gave him the appropriate amount of coin.

"Get us something to eat. We'll meet back here in ten minutes," he said, then promptly disappeared into the market down the street.

Zhi Lan scowled at his retreating form and walked into the market after him. A part of her didn't trust him to go off on his own, but she *was* hungry. And it probably wasn't smart to thieve on an empty stomach.

After purchasing two green onion pancakes from a nearby vendor and devouring hers in less than a minute, Zhi Lan spotted a market stall stocked with pots of pigment and brushes. She thought of Master Dan. His brown pigment *was* almost gone—she hadn't lied about that in her letter.

Zhi Lan approached the stall. A fresh-faced young man in blue robes beamed at her from behind his wares.

"Anything here that interests you, young miss?" the stall owner asked. "I have pigments from fresh roses that will complement your complexion." He gestured to the pots of pinks and rouges on one side of the stand.

"Do you have cinnabar brown?" Zhi Lan said.

The stall owner smiled wider. "I do believe your eyes and brows are arresting as they are."

Zhi Lan blushed and fidgeted. She never could handle such bold-faced market flattery, even if she knew it was all to make a sale. "It's to paint with, sir."

"Indeed!" He moved to the other side of the stand with the painting supplies. "Are you an artist, miss?"

"My master is," she said automatically. Then hastily added, "But I hope to be, someday."

"A protege, then!" the young stall owner said. "Very well. I do have the color you're looking for. A mixture of umber and cinnabar for a dimensional brown." He procured a stick of pigment and set it before her.

Zhi Lan rummaged in her bag, taking out a square of paper. "May I test it?"

"By all means," the stall owner said obligingly.

He scraped the surface of the stick with a knife, letting the pigment dust collect into a small porcelain dish. Then, he dripped in water until the powder became a dark brown liquid. He gave Zhi Lan a brush from his stand.

Zhi Lan accepted it gratefully. Her nerves calmed as she swirled the brush into the dish and dragged it over her paper, creating a rich, reddish brown stroke. The mark reminded Zhi Lan of a segment of bamboo. She continued with this idea, filling in the rest of the bamboo stalk and its branching leaves.

"The young miss is as talented as she is beautiful," the stall owner observed. "Is the pigment to your liking?"

"It is, thank you," Zhi Lan said. It was lovely and smooth, the quality on par with the pigments Master Dan liked to use. She rummaged for her coin purse. "How much?"

The stall owner told her the price. Zhi Lan counted her money, dismayed to find that she was only a few coins short.

"That seems a bit overpriced," she finally said.

The stall owner's eyes sparkled. "On the contrary. I only sell premium pigments. My price for something of this quality is quite low."

This was the usual push and pull of marketplace haggling. Zhi Lan never had the zest for it like some aunties she knew, but she was competent.

"I've seen better prices in Zhu City."

"Ah, but you're in Yun City now, young miss."

"Will you lower the price seeing as I'm a first-time customer?"

"Young miss seems to be traveling. I'm afraid you'll be an only-time customer."

Zhi Lan continued wheedling him, going from flattery to flirtation to borderline insult. The stall owner remained unmoved. She was starting to run out of cards to play.

At last, she drew in a slow breath. "I'll paint for you."

The stall owner raised a brow. "Oh?"

Zhi Lan pushed the bamboo painting she had done

toward him. "You may keep this and display it as a demon-stration of your product. I'm willing to do another, if you prefer."

"A trade of service," the stall owner mused. He took the painting with two fingers, holding it up to the light. "Yes. I am amenable to this proposal."

Zhi Lan breathed out. "Perfect. I'll—"

An arm reached past her and placed a smattering of cop-per coins on the stand. Zhi Lan turned around.

Shao Qing stood with a bundle of green fabric under his arm. Wordlessly, he took the cinnabar pigment stick and turned on his heel. Zhi Lan apologized profusely to the sur-prised stall owner, emptied the rest of her coin purse into his hand, and ran after Shao Qing before he disappeared into the crowd.

"He was willing to lower the price if I did a painting for him!" Zhi Lan said breathlessly when she made it to his side. She waved her empty coin purse before his face. "Now we have no money!"

Shao Qing barely flinched. He took the green onion pan-cake in her hand and began to eat. "He was willing to lower the price for a picture of bamboo?"

Zhi Lan didn't appreciate his dismissive tone. "Yes."

"Bamboo isn't anything special."

"Paintings make everything special. They're interpreta-tions of the world, not replicas," she insisted. "An artist can coax the beauty out of the most common objects."

Zhi Lan herself didn't appreciate the stately, dignified lines of bamboo until she attempted to translate them into brushstrokes on paper. Nor the graceful fan of a sparrow's wings. Nor the silly plumes on her own chicken, Pu'er. Paintings took the small, lovely things an artist observed and emphasized them for all the world to see.

Shao Qing didn't seem as if he understood.

Zhi Lan made an impatient noise. "In any case I was making great progress haggling until you interrupted me."

"Why bother haggling? It's unlikely a businessman would take anything less than what he intends to sell his products for."

"Have you ever shopped at a market?" Zhi Lan asked, aghast. "Haggling is the norm."

"It's pointless to go through all that effort only to save a few coins."

"Money is difficult to come by."

"There's nothing easier to come by than money," Shao Qing countered.

Zhi Lan thought that was rich coming from a thief who had just spent *her* money. "Only because you come by it unfairly! Other people labor and sweat for their coin. You reap the profits without any of the work."

"I labor and sweat during a heist. Is that not work?" Shao Qing said. "One could argue a magistrate sitting in his manor reaps profit without labor."

"A magistrate enforces order and justice in his city!"

"His constables enforce order and justice. And the magistrate you left seems to care more about being slighted than doing his job. The one we're going to now engages in illegal transactions."

"Do you take pleasure in having no principles?" Zhi Lan cried, stamping her foot.

"Principles can only make one's life more difficult and blind you to truth," Shao Qing said with his usual sangfroid. "You're willing to steal to retain your position. There are easier ways for a woman like you to get what she wants."

Zhi Lan scowled darkly. "And what ways would that be?"

He didn't seem to take her tone as a threat. "Simple. Become Magistrate Bu's concubine and you'll be drowning in fortune for the rest of your life."

"It's that easy, isn't it?" she said bitterly.

"Yes, it is."

"If you were a woman, would you marry for wealth?"

"Of course. It's the smart thing to do."

Zhi Lan's blood felt hot to the point of boiling. No doubt the scoundrel thought he was being helpful. But what made her even angrier was that Shao Qing was right. If the end goal was fortune, the smart thing to do *would* be to marry—or even become a rich man's concubine, his "little wife". But Zhi Lan was unwilling to give herself to a man in exchange for wealth and comfort.

Many would call her stupid for such a decision. It wasn't practical. It wasn't realistic. She was doing herself a disservice. And yet, Zhi Lan had principles. She knew betraying her own principles would truly be doing herself a disservice. She had seen too many women get burned going down the practical path, living out the rest of their lives with men they disliked, or men who only cared for their beauty. If Zhi Lan were to marry, it would be for love, not fortune. She would rather suffer discomfort in her body than in her soul.

But a part of her wished she didn't have principles, or that they were different. That she could've done the practical thing when she was given the opportunity to.

Five years ago, a nobleman had passed through her village. It had been an unfruitful year in the fields due to drought, and Ma had been pregnant with her fourth child. The days were miserable, but Ma, with her cheerful nature, tried her best to lift everyone's spirits. She'd made puppets out of fallen chicken feathers for her brothers and let Zhi Lan put on a bit of her rouge—a luxury Ma herself rarely indulged in.

Zhi Lan had wandered out that day with flushed cheeks and lips, her spirits marginally lifted. She didn't realize she had caught the passing nobleman's eye until he waved an imperious hand out the window of his carriage. Zhi Lan noted his silk brocade sleeve and stopped, wondering what an older man of such importance would want with her.

He had asked her to come home with him and become one of his concubines. Zhi Lan had only been fifteen—and refused him staunchly.

The nobleman, undeterred, followed her back to her cottage, hoping her parents would give a different answer. But Ma and Ba bravely turned him away. He had left in a huff.

Their neighbors watched this all from their windows, and later, one auntie had come by to say that Zhi Lan had been quite foolish indeed.

"Your girl is of age to be married anyway! Why not to a rich man? It would be a blessing to have such high connections during these hard times!"

Her parents would hear none of it.

For the next month, there was hardly enough food on the table. Ma lost the baby. Zhi Lan had been racked with guilt. Some days she wondered where her family would be if she had accepted the nobleman's offer. They'd be living in the city, dressed in silk instead of hemp, with their bellies full every day regardless of whether it rained or not. She would have an extra sibling.

Ma and Ba told her to stop lingering on such thoughts.

"Why bear the guilt? You didn't cause the drought. Unless you are secretly the Dragon King and withheld rain from us," Ma had joked. She placed her hand on her belly in a sad, wistful sort of way. "This child was not meant to be. Perhaps it will find us in its next life."

"No daughter of mine will be a concubine to some lecherous old weasel!" Ba exclaimed. "We villagers work for everything we have. We reap our own rewards. We bear our own losses. Hold on to that pride, Lan'er."

Guilt was like an ink stain on a white sleeve. One could wash most of it away, but traces of it would still linger. Zhi Lan had learned to forgive herself, to stand with her principles. To be proud, like her Baba said.

But grim thoughts always lurked in the back of her mind. How long could she continue on as a painter's apprentice, hardly making any income at all? What if her pursuits crashed and burned and there was no other path to take? She would've been better off marrying that nobleman after all.

And now look where my principles have brought me, Zhi Lan thought dryly, stopping before the walls of Magistrate

Li's manor. They had made it back a little before noon. The passersby were sparser than before. Shao Qing shook out the green bundle in his arm, revealing two roughspun robes.

"Why green? Isn't black standard for thieving?" Zhi Lan asked.

"It's daytime. Black is as conspicuous as white. Green will blend into the foliage." Shao Qing offered the smaller one to her.

Zhi Lan held the fabric up to the willow tree sticking out of the walls. "But this isn't even the right shade!"

Whereas the willow leaves were bright and sprightly, the robes Shao Qing had picked out were a dull olive.

"I can't tell," Shao Qing said.

Zhi Lan huffed and shook her head. Being angry at him was a waste of energy. Besides, what did *he* know of being a woman? She slipped on the olive robe and tightened the fabric belt. Shao Qing did the same.

The front gates of the manor creaked open. Zhi Lan scrambled back, her heart leaping to her throat. Shao Qing placed a hand on her shoulder and steered them to the adjacent wall, where they could peek out without being spotted.

"Don't act guilty before you've committed the crime," he murmured into her ear. The gesture was unintentionally intimate.

Zhi Lan tried not to notice how his breath tickled her cheek. "This isn't a crime," she whispered back. She was technically taking back Master Dan's painting on his behalf. It was justified. But the longer she stood there, the less it felt like justice.

The guards at the gate were chatting with a group of servants. Zhi Lan was too far away to hear what they were saying. Shao Qing squeezed her shoulder.

"Let's go," he said.

"Go where?"

He looked up. Zhi Lan followed his gaze.

"Over the wall."

10

A DISTRACTED GUARD WAS A thief's best friend. That was the first lesson Yao had taught him.

As the guards before Magistrate Li's manor were chatting, Shao Qing counted enough footholds in the wall to get himself onto the roof. Just like Magistrate Bu's manor, the west wall was covered in flourishing vines.

"I don't know how to climb," Zhi Lan whispered, a panicked note in her voice.

Shao Qing produced the coil of rope he had hidden around his middle. He had snagged an abandoned clothesline after purchasing the green robes, looping one end around his hips and wrapping the rest around his torso. He unfurled it now.

Zhi Lan stood very still as he slipped the other end around her waist and secured it with a sturdy knot.

"When I make it to the roof, climb up after me," Shao Qing said.

"What part of *I don't know how to climb* did you not understand?"

"Hold onto the rope and brace your feet against the wall."

Shao Qing wedged his foot into a deep crack in the stone, tested the strength of the vines above him, and began his ascent. His senses sharpened as he went through the familiar exercise of finding a foothold and pulling himself up. He reached the top in a few minutes. Flattening himself against the roof of the west house, the boughs of a willow tree brushing his back, Shao Qing peered down at Zhi Lan, motioning for her to follow.

She looked as if she wanted to run, but after a moment, seemed to steel herself and grip the rope. Shao Qing watched her unsteady ascent for what felt like hours. Her hands finally appeared over the eaves. He pulled her up and Zhi Lan flopped gracelessly on her belly beside him, scraping the tile with her feet and panting like she was starved for air.

She was the worst thief he'd ever seen. Shao Qing wondered if they were going to make it out of this alive. Though he had to admit, the threat of possible death made this rather enticing.

Shao Qing turned and assessed the front courtyard. Servants ran to and fro, carrying buckets of steaming water to the main wing—most likely for a bath. Some were sweeping away the fallen willow leaves from the winding stone path in the garden. No one glanced up, too busy with their menial tasks. The masters of the house seemed to be within the rooms.

Shao Qing shifted onto his feet and walked silently along the ridge of the roof to the main house, keeping low. It was

likely anything precious would be
stored there. This was no planned
heist—he could only act on his own instincts. Zhi Lan followed close behind, still
sounding short of breath.

"Let's go down," Shao Qing said once they were on top of the main house.

"How?" Zhi Lan whispered.

Shao Qing glanced at yet another willow tree behind them. There was a convenient branch a foot away from the roof. It looked sturdy enough to bear their weight.

She paled. "There's no way."

"It's the only way."

There were fewer servants in the back courtyard. Shao Qing waited until they cleared before he straightened and stepped onto the tree. Zhi Lan buried her face into her hands and took a deep breath before following suit. She wobbled violently on the branch as she placed one foot in front of the other.

Shao Qing reached forward to steady her, but a loose piece of bark rolled beneath his feet.

In the next second, he was falling, the ground hurtling toward him and the wind rushing past his limbs.

All at once, the rope around his middle yanked taut, halting his fall with bruising force. The breath was squeezed from his lungs. Shao Qing managed to look up through the momentary pain.

Zhi Lan straddled the branch above him, clinging onto the rope that connected them so tightly her knuckles were white. He hung suspended from her hold alone. She was stronger than he'd suspected. Shao Qing motioned for her to lower him, but she shook her head vehemently.

He looked down.

A servant girl passed by with a bucket of water. Shao Qing dangled directly above her head.

He had been inordinately clumsy. Usually his feet were steady, but he wasn't entirely displeased with this turn of events. The back of his neck tingled. Color bloomed at the edge of his desaturated vision. Anticipation was the best part of thieving—whether he would get away or get caught. It sent his pulse racing.

The girl stopped, then turned in a confused circle. Hanging on the precipice of suspense sent a rush of blood through his limbs. He held his breath until he grew lightheaded.

At last, the servant girl shrugged and went back through the front courtyard. When she disappeared, the rope around Shao Qing's waist slackened and he landed heavily on his feet. Above him, Zhi Lan blew on her hands, shaking out her wrists.

Shao Qing brushed himself off and straightened. He motioned for Zhi Lan to come down.

"How?" she mouthed.

He held out his arms.

After a hesitant glance, Zhi Lan lowered herself so she was dangling from the branch by her hands, then plummeted unceremoniously into him. He managed to catch her shoulders and one of her legs. She resembled an ungraceful heap of wrinkled fabric, leaves, and rope.

Shao Qing set her down.

"Don't make me do that again," she wheezed.

He unknotted the rope from his waist. After Zhi Lan did the same, he shoved the coil underneath a stone statue of a miniature pavilion.

They had landed before the main house, a precarious position. A long veranda stretched down like a hallway, doors on the left and the open courtyard on the right. He recalled Yao's map. The magistrate's study should be in the center of the building.

"Follow my lead," he said to Zhi Lan. "Quietly."

Down the veranda they went, ducking beneath open windows and slipping past ajar doors.

Shao Qing counted the numerous rooms, walking toward the one close to the center. He pressed his ear against the screen door. Silence. A film of dust coated the threshold, unlike the clean polished wood of the others. There was a lock on the door, but not the window. He pushed it open and quickly climbed inside, holding the frame open for Zhi Lan to scramble in.

The room was dim, the air stale and stagnant. Unoccupied, as he suspected. The walls were bare and the porcelain vases empty. White sheets covered the tables and chairs. There was an old baby crib pushed to the corner where a bed should've been.

Not a place for art, then.

"I don't like this." Zhi Lan's eyes darted around the white walls and sheets. "It looks like a room for the deceased."

Shao Qing touched her elbow to steer her away from the screen window. She let out a startled squeak.

"It's just an extra room," Shao Qing said. "The rich have too many to put all of them to use." He meant to be reassuring, but he couldn't help feeling a hint of amusement at her reaction.

Zhi Lan swallowed, her gaze straying to the crib. "Do you think...this room is for the missing child? What if its spirit is watching us?"

So she was worried about the silly story An Qin had told.

"Focus," Shao Qing said. "We're here for your painting."

Zhi Lan nodded, but there was a crease between her brows that he had a sudden urge to smooth away. This, he ignored.

"The magistrate's study should be the room behind this wall," he said in a low voice, walking to the far end of the room. He pressed his ear against the wall, straining to hear any movement. Nothing.

Shao Qing waited for another minute before deeming it safe. He and Zhi Lan managed to slip out of the window again and head a few steps down the veranda.

The door to the magistrate's study was wide open. And luckily, empty.

Or so Shao Qing thought. They made it five steps in when he realized there was someone behind the grand desk to the right of the entrance.

A distinguished-looking gentleman was reclined in a chair, his head tipped back, his broad chin covered with a gray goatee. His lined faced looked just past middle-aged. A loud snore emitted from him. Judging from his age and fine dress, Shao Qing guessed that this was Magistrate Li himself. On his desk was an open scroll—a painting of a waterfall.

Shao Qing padded silently behind a silk screen on the other side of the room, pulling Zhi Lan with him. The top two thirds was silk stretched across a wooden frame painted with cherry blossoms, the lower third was intricately carved wood, stained a deep brown.

Zhi Lan turned around, looking at him with wide eyes. "That's the painting. Do we just grab it?" she whispered.

He shook his head and pressed a finger over his lips. Caution and patience were required now. Untried thieves always got sloppy with their target in sight. It would be ridiculously easy to grab the painting from underneath the magistrate's nose—and very risky. Normally he would be tempted to try something reckless, but with Zhi Lan here, he figured he should err on the side of caution. He assessed their position. There was a large, bright window behind them. If the magistrate were to wake, he would easily see their forms silhouetted behind the screen.

"Get down," Shao Qing said, his voice barely a whisper. He crouched to the floor and laid himself down so he was concealed by the lower third of the screen. Zhi Lan squatted awkwardly beside him.

Someone knocked loudly on the doorframe. Shao Qing grabbed Zhi Lan's arm and pulled her toward him. She landed with a soft "oof" against his chest, her uneven breath tickling his chin. The two froze when Magistrate Li grunted, startling awake.

"Hm, who's there?"

Zhi Lan grabbed a fistful of Shao Qing's robe.

"Your bath is drawn, my lord," a servant's voice came from outside.

"Ah. I'll be there in a minute." Shuffling ensued from behind the screen.

Shao Qing held his breath. Zhi Lan was still clinging onto him like her life depended on it. He felt the press of her forehead against his neck.

A short chuckle came from Magistrate Li. "Ah. An excellent painting."

Then, more shuffling and grunts.

It seemed an eternity before they heard the magistrate's heavy footsteps.

"After you, my lord," the servant said.

A soft whoosh of wind blew into the room, bringing in warm afternoon air and lifting Zhi Lan's scent to Shao Qing. He turned his head ever so slightly, his nose brushing against her hair.

His heart beat faster.

The door shut and the footsteps faded, leaving the room in silence. Shao Qing touched Zhi Lan's back, intending for the gesture as a sign to get up. But his hand lingered, splaying over the dip of her waist. He was suddenly aware of the slight curves pressed against his chest and the weight of her hips on top of his. He had never found such things pleasing, but this...

Zhi Lan lifted her head, her delicate brows furrowed in question.

She mouthed a series of silent words. Shao Qing wasn't sure what she was saying—only that the pink of her lips was the most vibrant color he had seen in a while.

She suddenly smacked his chest. "*I asked is it clear?*" she hissed.

Shao Qing paused. Then nodded.

Zhi Lan removed herself from his person immediately, her cheeks flushed the same pink as her lips. He sat up as she slipped around the screen to where Magistrate Li had been a minute earlier. Shao Qing followed without thinking. All he knew was that he wasn't quite done looking at her yet. He wondered what had gotten into him.

Zhi Lan unfurled the scroll which Magistrate Li had closed before leaving, her face flooding with relief. "It really is the one," she said, clutching it to her chest and letting out a sigh. Her eyes seemed to shine when she regarded him. "Thank you."

Shao Qing nodded. He wasn't sure whether the sudden rush to his head was due to the theft, or...

His gaze strayed past Zhi Lan's shoulder. A small scroll hung from the wall, the image catching his eye.

A painting of a dragon among clouds.

Shao Qing was walking forward before he knew it.

"What are you doing?" Zhi Lan hissed.

He unhooked the painting and studied it. The dragon had floating whiskers and sapphire claws, its mighty body twisting between wisps of mist. Nothing marked it as any different from the other dragon paintings he had come across.

But Shao Qing had never felt this way around any of them.

What if his sudden rush of emotions hadn't been because of Zhi Lan? What if it had been his soul, calling to him? Perhaps it had known she would lead him to it, which explained why he'd been drawn to her.

A shiver ran down Shao Qing's spine as Zhi Lan grabbed his forearm. "I hear footsteps," she said in a panicked voice. "Let's hide. Or better yet, let's go."

He rolled up the dragon painting and tucked it into the pouch at his waist.

At that moment, the door swung open and Magistrate Li stepped into the room. His gaze locked on Shao Qing with odd familiarity.

"Wen Jun?" the magistrate said in confusion. "How did you…?" Then his gaze fell on Zhi Lan, and the scroll clutched in her hand. His eyes widened when he looked back at Shao Qing, this time with alarm. "You're thieves!"

Just as Magistrate Li hollered for guards, Shao Qing grabbed Zhi Lan's wrist. They barreled past the magistrate, following the garden path studded with shrubs and rock sculptures that led to a pavilion suspended over a picturesque pond of floating lily pads. They made it underneath the shaded structure, panting.

From this vantage point, Shao Qing noticed that the pond led out to a patch of wilderness overgrown with trees and bamboo. There was no back wall in sight. He didn't know how far the magistrate's security extended, but it was their only way out.

The shouts of guards followed. A handful of them charged toward the pavilion, their heavy armor clinking. Shao Qing halted at the railing, peering down at the murky pond below them. He couldn't tell how deep it went. There was no time to find out.

"Can you swim?" Shao Qing asked Zhi Lan.

"Yes but—"

He grabbed her around the waist and swung her over the railing. She shrieked. A loud splash followed. Shao Qing barreled into the water after her. His feet hit the bottom of the pond.

Zhi Lan was a few paces ahead, paddling toward the bamboo wilderness with impressive speed, the scroll shoved down the back of her collar. The further they swam, the deeper the water got.

Spears splashed on either side of Shao Qing as the guards attempted to attack from afar. They were encumbered by their armor and could not jump into the water after them.

"Wait, wait! Don't hurt them!" Magistrate Li shouted. "Bring the boy back alive!"

Shao Qing took the opportunity to submerge fully, kicking his feet as he propelled himself through the murky water. His lungs and muscles burned. It seemed an eternity before he broke the surface. By then, the magistrate's pavilion had grown smaller. The guards gathered at the railing, seeming to have chosen not to pursue them.

A strange choice, but Shao Qing didn't linger on it.

The rocky shore came into view. Zhi Lan pulled herself from the water, pond weeds clinging to her drenched hair. Her skirt hung heavy and wet, leaving a trail of puddles as she hurried to take cover in the shrubbery. Shao Qing clambered after her, shivering and lightheaded, less from the cold and more from the scroll at his waist.

He pressed a hand to it, feeling the solid wooden rods and the thickness of the silk brocade. Could it be what he thought it was?

11

ZHI LAN WAS DRENCHED IN pond muck. Her clothes were heavy and stuck unpleasantly to her skin. There was something slippery in her shoes. She was out of breath and shivering.

And skies, she was probably a wanted criminal now.

Zhi Lan stumbled to a halt when she made it to a small clearing. They were in a patch of wilderness, though she could tell it didn't extend very far by the sight of buildings speckling the distance through the trees. She fumbled for Master Dan's painting, which she had shoved into the back of her collar right before Shao Qing had flung her into the water.

Her hands trembled, dread roiling in her gut when she found the silk brocade wet to the touch. When she unrolled it, her stomach dropped.

Every meticulous detail Master Dan had layered on was gone, dissolved into dark, blue green splotches. The red signature stamp, too, was illegible. All that was left was a hazy landscape of bleeding pigments.

Zhi Lan's breath hitched. "It's ruined!"

The sneaking, the climbing, the running—all that for nothing! How was she supposed to face Master Dan now?

Zhi Lan broke into a sob at the thought of her poor master. He had spent three months on this masterpiece, yet the pond water had washed it all away in minutes. She'd always thought art was eternal in the way it was meticulously preserved, passing from teacher to student. Yet here was the truth before her—art was nothing more than ink on silk, fragile and transient.

Shao Qing stood at her periphery, wringing out his sleeves. She turned to him.

"What were you thinking?" Zhi Lan demanded shrilly, shaking the ruined painting in his face. He hardly blinked at the violent motion, instead stepping away to remove his outer robe and drape it on a nearby branch. "Couldn't you have waited for me to put it somewhere safe?"

Still nothing. Zhi Lan watched, utterly appalled at the calm manner in which he removed the dragon painting he had stolen from a bag at his hip and unrolled it.

It was a small handheld scroll, on which an ink washed dragon curled across paper. The painting was dry.

Shao Qing studied it for a beat, tracing his finger over the lines. He held it to his chest.

Then in a sudden motion, he flung it hard enough that it splashed back into the water they had just come from.

"What. Did. You. Just. Do?" Zhi Lan hardly recognized

her voice, dark and guttural with anger. Her muscles hurt. She felt hot and cold all at once. "You had a waterproof bag all this time, and you used it on a painting you didn't even want?"

Shao Qing finally turned around. She expected him to defend himself, to be as jittery and angry as she was. But he looked as if he hadn't felt the effects of anything. Not the swim, not the chase. Not her anger. Like a wooden puppet whose strings had been cut, Shao Qing collapsed on the debris covered ground, his legs splayed before him. His eyes were blank. So terribly blank.

Zhi Lan knelt before him and pushed his shoulder. "I asked you a question," she said, her vision blurring with tears. "Answer me!"

Nothing.

There was something unnatural about him. He was like a still pond, but no matter how many rocks Zhi Lan threw at him, his surface did not break.

"Demon," Zhi Lan whispered hoarsely. "There is something wrong with you."

She wanted to shake herself for being so foolish. She should have never left Master Dan. Now, she was stuck in another city with a thief. They were both probably wanted criminals. Magistrate Li and his guards had seen their faces. She couldn't go to anyone else for help without risking arrest.

Zhi Lan clenched her clammy hands, fighting the tears welling in her eyes. She had no idea where she was. She had no money. The clothes on her back were not fit to be seen. Her escort seemed to have stopped functioning entirely.

What was she going to *do*?

Panic clenched like a fist around her throat, but Zhi Lan clung desperately to the last shred of sense she had. Ma and Ba had taught her to keep her head in the most dire of situations. Like during the month they had starved. Like when Ma had lost the baby. If her family could rise resilient to such hardships, so could she.

Shao Qing, with all his oddities, had gotten her this far. Even if he were a demon, Zhi Lan refused to believe that he was without honor.

A red pouch stuck out from the folds of his inner robe. It was the sentimental ornament he held. Sentiment was human, as far as Zhi Lan knew. Without thinking, she grabbed it from him.

Shao Qing looked up sharply, as if the pouch were a magnet and he couldn't help but be drawn to it. "What are you doing?"

Zhi Lan squeezed the pouch in her hand, pond water dribbling down her wrist. "Tell me about this."

A crease appeared between his brows, and he looked away. "Why are you still here? We've finished our bargain, haven't we?"

"You need to escort me back to Zhu City."

If she were doomed, at the very least she should go back and be there for Master Dan.

Now, to shake some sense into her escort.

Shao Qing leaned forward and tucked his legs underneath him, his movements stiff, as if he had just regained control over his limbs. "You can go back without me."

"I don't know the way. If you don't tell me what's wrong with you, I'm going to throw this pouch into the pond."

"Back with your threats?"

Zhi Lan couldn't describe the relief she felt in this exchange. He was back to normal. Or at least as normal as he could be. The emptiness, though not completely gone, gave way to his usual cool detachedness that was more human than anything else about him.

"Why do you want to know?" Shao Qing finally said.

"You clearly suffer from some sort of...condition. You fumbled our bargain. I deserve to know why."

Shao Qing looked at her. She couldn't tell if he was thinking, or if his mind was merely blank.

"Fine." He stood up slowly. "Let's start walking."

The two, still dripping wet, continued deeper into the trees.

Zhi Lan supposed the beginning would be a good place to start. Had he always been this way? She drew in a shaky breath. "What were the circumstances of your birth?"

Shao Qing glanced at her for a moment. She wondered if she had been too rude in her questioning before he finally spoke. "I was found in the back of a pleasure house. They say my mother was one of the courtesans there, but no one would claim me so I was sent to the orphanage as an infant."

"Were you treated well there?" Zhi Lan ventured to ask. She wanted to keep him talking, terrified that he would revert back to an inanimate puppet like before.

He shook his head. "There was never enough to eat and we were put to work, harvesting silk from silkworms."

Zhi Lan blinked rapidly, wiping the pond water out of her eyes. "I thought orphanages were supposed to take care of children until they were adopted."

"Adoption is rare in Zhu City. Most prefer to raise their own. And the children who leave the orphanage with a guardian are likely to be servants...or worse." He said all this without feeling. Zhi Lan was almost afraid of what else he was going to reveal.

"So you spent your childhood there?"

"Not all of it. I ran away."

She nodded slowly. "Then you joined a band of thieves?"

"Not immediately." His pale gaze slid to the red pouch in Zhi Lan's hand, which she had held onto since Shao Qing never made a move to take it back. "I had a little sister, Su Su."

Zhi Lan held her breath. So that was who he had been apologizing to in his sleep.

"She was found in the same place I was, three years after me. Perhaps we were blood-related, perhaps not. Either way, we had kinship, and we took to each other," Shao Qing said. "Su Su had a sickly constitution. The winters in the orphanage were harsh, the rules were strict, and the hours we worked only made her worse. I knew she wouldn't survive for long if we went on."

"You ran away with her for her sake?" Zhi Lan asked gently.

"That was what I told myself. But it was a selfish decision. I ran away because I chafed under the rules, and I thought there were better things waiting for me. That I could feed and clothe us better than the orphanage could."

"How old were you?"

"Thirteen."

Mere children on the streets of an expansive city. Zhi Lan thought of her own childhood, of the fields and rolling hills, of the rivers and houses that held well-meaning adults and her own caring family. She had never been without protection or warmth when she was that young. Children were not meant to suffer so.

Zhi Lan fidgeted with the pouch in her hands, shivering. Her clothes were still wet, but their walking warmed her limbs. "How did you manage?"

Shao Qing shrugged. "We begged and we stole. It was difficult for me to find a respectable job—no one trusted a lone child. Without money, we slept on the streets. But I was too proud to go back to the orphanage. Su Su didn't want to return either...though, perhaps she was only humoring me." He said all this with cold composure, as if the story didn't affect him at all. "Eventually the proprietor of an herbalist shop took pity on me and let me be his errand boy. For a time I was making enough to feed Su Su and myself, though not enough for permanent shelter. I thought we were living grandly. Our stomachs were full, we slept under the stars, and we could go wherever we pleased."

"That's good," Zhi Lan said softly.

"Su Su thought I was..." Shao Qing let out a mirthless laugh. "She thought I was her hero."

"Of course. You rescued her from the orphanage and took care of her, like any good brother would."

He did not disagree with her, but he didn't look like he agreed, either. "My foolishness caught up with me. My employer was generous and often I ended the day with more coin than we needed to spend. Su Su was eager to help, so I let her keep our money safe while I worked."

Shao Qing's eyes slid to the red pouch in Zhi Lan's hands. The accessory suddenly felt heavy.

"There were other boys on the street who decided we were easy targets. They took everything we had. Including Su Su's life," he said shortly. "I saw it happen but I was too afraid to stop them."

Zhi Lan sucked in a breath.

"Money is so easily acquired," Shao Qing said. "Yet Su Su sacrificed herself for a few coins."

Tears burned at the back of Zhi Lan's eyes. She couldn't help them—it was a tragic story.

"I should've been consumed by thoughts of revenge after that. Any man would," Shao Qing said. "But I barely remember those boys. It wasn't revenge that drove me mad. It was grief. Regret. I resented myself. I wished that I hadn't been a coward."

"Shao Qing..."

He kept his gaze forward. "You don't want to hear the story anymore?"

Zhi Lan shook her head. "Continue."

"I went to the bamboo forest at the outskirts of Zhu City one day. I met a demon. A bamboo spirit."

A shiver ran down Zhi Lan's spine at the mention of such monsters. Demons were notorious for preying on humans, making bargains and stealing their essence. It was the only way they'd be able to cultivate into immortals, or so the folktales say.

"What did it say to you?" Zhi Lan asked.

"That if I gave it my soul, I wouldn't be afraid anymore. So I did."

"What?"

"The numbness was better than grief. I felt free. My soul was a burden."

"Your soul is not a burden, it's what makes you human!" Zhi Lan said, aghast. She was horrified by his admission. He must've truly resented himself to willingly do such a thing. She halted in her tracks. "The way you acted back there, it was because you're soulless? You were gone for a moment. You looked like a puppet, a husk of a person! How is this *good*?"

Shao Qing hadn't stopped walking, so Zhi Lan was forced to catch up to him.

"There are drawbacks," he said calmly, as if they were chatting about tea. "Colors are duller. Food tastes like dust. Sometimes I can sit for hours and forget where I am."

Zhi Lan was bewildered. She suddenly saw Shao Qing in a new light. A foolish boy. A frightened child. A grieving brother. Someone who loved and grieved to such an acute, painful point that he had rid himself of his feelings entirely. Now, he was a soulless man.

Yet he didn't seem entirely lost.

"You still...function," Zhi Lan said. "How is that possible?"

"I sometimes wonder that myself," Shao Qing admitted. "I feel it getting worse yearly. But when I joined Yao and his gang...the thieving made me feel alive again. Danger brings me back to myself. Somewhat."

"Is that why you stole that dragon painting back there?" Zhi Lan demanded. "To *feel* something?"

Shao Qing studied the forest floor. "I've had dreams every night that my soul was in a painting of a dragon," he said slowly. "Two days ago, when I met you, I felt something change. I'm not sure what it was. But it must have something to do with the painting."

"The demon took your soul. Why would it be in a painting?"

"Perhaps that's where the demon chose to keep it. I've attempted to find it a few times before. I've been unsuccessful."

"So you've been looking for your soul all this time?"

Shao Qing gazed blankly at the scenery before them. "I suppose it's an interesting challenge."

Zhi Lan frowned. "The only reason you're trying to find your soul is because it's challenging?"

Shao Qing merely shrugged.

Zhi Lan's mind whirled with this information. She doubted he could give a true answer in his current state. A body was meant to have a soul, just as a painting was meant to hold meaning. A part of Shao Qing must know this, however subconsciously. Perhaps that was why he wanted to look for his soul—to restore the balance within him.

"I'm sorry," she finally said. "You've suffered greatly."

He glanced over at her. There was nothing much behind that gaze, but it only made her feel worse.

"Maybe I can find your soul, if you haven't had the luck." The words were out of her mouth before she could stop them.

Shao Qing stopped in his tracks. Zhi Lan turned to face him, feeling feverish and reckless.

Guilt and grief were not easy feelings to sit with. They had weighed upon her like stones ever since she refused that nobleman's offer all those years ago. Zhi Lan's situation was nowhere near as tragic as Shao Qing's, but at the very least, she had the support of her loved ones.

Shao Qing had no one.

She understood why he would want numbness over grief. But to lose grief was to lose love, and that was a steep price to pay.

They had reached the edge of the forest, the trees falling away to an open expanse of city. Zhi Lan held the red pouch in one hand and Master Dan's ruined painting in the other. She had nothing left to lose. Perhaps if she couldn't save herself, she could save someone else.

"What do you want in return?" Shao Qing finally said.

"Nothing." Zhi Lan pushed the wet hair out of her face. "This isn't a transaction."

Shao Qing had helped her all this time. She wanted to return the favor even if she didn't have to—even if nothing came of it. She was not entirely without manners, after all.

"Why, then?"

"Because *I* have a soul."

He shook his head slowly. "Does having a soul make you that foolish?"

"I'm only trying to help," she said hoarsely.

Shao Qing walked toward the city, not bothering to look at her as he said, "Save your effort. You should worry about yourself."

Zhi Lan glanced down, assessing the objects in her hands

and her disheveled clothing. Her throat tightened, the sting of his words sobering her.

Ma had always said to leave broken men to their own fate—that there was no one who could fix them but themselves. Zhi Lan knew this to be true, yet Shao Qing was in no condition to fix himself. He needed a push, and she was willing to give it.

Still, did she really have time to argue with a husk of a man who seemed almost content with his condition?

Zhi Lan drew in a breath and centered herself. Her first duty was to her master. She had gone on this journey for his sake, and she couldn't be side-tracked quite yet. Master Dan was waiting for her. She needed to hurry back and bear the consequences with him.

Zhi Lan pressed her lips into a grim line and followed Shao Qing into the city.

SHAO QING NEVER ONCE REGRETTED bargaining with the demon. Whether it was because he no longer possessed the ability to care, or because he truly was content with his state, he didn't know.

There were the drawbacks, of course, but he tolerated them well enough. He didn't have a strong desire to taste food or see color. He was satisfied with his peace. And when the stillness grew to be too much, he did something reckless.

Yet he felt something akin to regret during the journey back to Zhu City.

It wasn't because Magistrate Li's dragon painting hadn't been his soul. Finding it had become a game to him—a sport he never took seriously.

It was the way Zhi Lan treated him after she knew about his condition.

They continued on in their wet clothes, drawing odd looks from passersby. The noon sun dried their outer garments, and by late afternoon, they were presentable enough to ask for help.

A kind old farmer had taken them through the city gate on his mule-drawn cart. Their forged papers had gotten damp, but they were luckily still legible.

"Where are you youngsters off to?" the farmer asked cheerily from his seat at the front.

Zhi Lan didn't speak as Shao Qing expected, so the response fell to him.

"To the magistrate's," he said.

"Indeed? Well, expect it to be a long wait. I hear Magistrate Bu isn't seeing any petitioners until he finds a thief."

Shao Qing absorbed this information. He had almost forgotten he was a wanted man.

The farmer looked over his shoulder curiously. "What injustice has fallen upon you, if I may ask?"

Shao Qing kept his gaze downcast. Zhi Lan sat beside him, her face pale, looking small and withdrawn. She hardly seemed aware of the conversation they were having—an odd change to her usual animated self.

"A family matter. My wife prefers not to speak of it." Shao Qing put an arm around Zhi Lan's shoulders to get a reaction out of her, but she only stiffened slightly.

"I see," the farmer said, seemingly disappointed by the lack of gossip. "All the best to you. You are lucky to have each other, at least."

When the farmer stopped to procure sustenance for himself and his mule, Shao Qing slipped a couple of pork buns from a nearby vendor. He gave one of them to Zhi Lan. She took it and ate without even scolding him for stealing.

As the journey continued, she seemed to forget Shao Qing was there at all. She would reach for her bag, then startle when he gave it to her, like he was nothing but a ghostly presence. Shao Qing usually didn't mind being ignored. Avoiding perception was a good thing for a thief, but this discomfited him. It was as if Zhi Lan had decided he was less than human without his soul. That he was no longer worthy of acknowledgement.

The closer they got to Magistrate Bu's manor, the more acute his discomfort. If he were capable of more emotion, he was sure Zhi Lan's disregard would feel like a stab in the chest.

Finally when the white afternoon sun yielded to a gray dusk, the farmer dropped them off before Magistrate Bu's manor. Shao Qing stood, stretching his legs.

Towering beside the residence was the *yamen*, the place where the magistrate held court, solved disputes between citizens, and brought criminals to justice. The sweeping tiled eaves loomed over them ominously. Shao Qing had avoided stepping foot in its shadow for his entire criminal career.

A crowd gathered outside the gates now. An irritated man was ringing the bell outside repeatedly to request entrance, the loud peals clanging through the street.

Zhi Lan raised her voice to thank the old farmer—the first words she had said to him all day. He seemed surprised that she could speak after all, and heartily wished them luck as he drove his mule cart down the road.

Eventually, a guard stepped out from the *yamen* and barked a few sharp words. The crowd of disgruntled petitioners dispersed, moaning and complaining.

"Maybe he'll see us tomorrow," a man said hopefully.

"Bah. Not if the magistrate doesn't find that godforsaken thief. A thief, bold enough to steal from right under his nose! A man such as that would surely be out of the empire by now."

"What are common folk like us supposed to do but wait? We can only hope his lordship will oblige us soon."

The crowd washed over Shao Qing and Zhi Lan like a river past rocks, until the two of them were the only ones left in the street. When it was relatively quiet again, he turned to her, wanting to see her even as the sun waned and cast ashy shadows over her features.

"For what it's worth," Shao Qing said shortly. "I'm sorry."

Zhi Lan met his gaze with her piercing one. Her dark eyes glittered, deep and dangerous with mysterious intent. Shao Qing was suddenly drowning in them, unable to look away.

"I have decided," she said.

"You have decided...what?"

"That I'm going to find your soul."

Shao Qing blinked slowly, confused. Not this again. Why was she so adamant about finding his soul? "Worry about yourself. I don't want your help."

She scowled. "You may not want my help, but you *need* my help." She hugged her elbows, as if bracing herself for her next words. "And I owe you a debt. You inadvertently saved me, a few days ago. Magistrate Bu was making...unseemly advances and I prayed for a distraction. Then *you* came. It must have been divine intervention."

"It was not my intention to help you. You're only—"

"Don't bother telling me how stupid or foolish I am! I won't believe a single terrible thing you say to me. And I don't believe that you are terrible yourself. You didn't have to accompany me to Yun City, but you did."

He felt compelled to deny this. "You threatened me by calling the guards."

"You could have easily escaped during the night or any time during our journey," she countered, lifting her chin stubbornly. "And you gave those urchins my money. That's right. I noticed. There's something worth saving in that miserable body of yours. So, listen well. If I make it out of that manor alive, the first thing I'm doing is hunting down your unfeeling soul. You can stop your thieving and ridiculous antics and start preparing to face whatever lies in your heart. You can try and run, but I will find you, Shao Qing, thief and scoundrel. Even if I'm a ghost by tomorrow I will find you."

Zhi Lan grabbed his hand, her fingers small but insistent. Shao Qing's chest tightened inexplicably at the contact. She pressed Su Su's damp red pouch into his palm, then spun around and marched to the front gate.

Shao Qing watched her go, her robes white against the growing shadows. Only when he turned to leave did he realize that the gray of the evening had become a soft, purplish blue.

13

IN ITS SCROLL, THE DRAGON flicked its tail.

PART III
TO SWAY A SOUL

14

Z HI LAN SHOWED THE GUARDS at the manor gate her badge from Lady Bu, which luckily survived the ordeal at the pond. She was let in without comment.

In the courtyard, servants rushed to and fro, preparing for the evening meal. No one paid her any mind as Zhi Lan slipped into her room.

She was relieved to find everything as she left it.

Zhi Lan quickly changed into clean clothes. Regretfully, there was no time for a bath to wash the pond scum off of her skin, so she settled with splashing her face and raking a comb through her hair. After grabbing the cinnabar brown pigment she had bought and the ruined painting of Shui Jin Mountain, she knocked on Master Dan's door that adjoined her own room.

Her heart was at her throat as she waited.

What if he wasn't there? What if Magistrate Bu had sent him to the gallows, or shut him up in some sort of torture chamber? Her poor, scholarly master would never survive such cruel tactics.

Her racing thoughts quieted when Master Dan's voice came from within.

"Come in."

Zhi Lan exhaled and pushed the door open.

Master Dan sat behind his desk, a brush in hand and a painting before him. His white robes were neat and there wasn't a hair on his head out of place. The sight was so comforting and familiar she almost wept. It felt like an eternity since she'd last seen him.

He raised his eyebrows at her entrance. "Zhi Lan. I thought you finally listened to me and left."

"I would never leave you, Master Dan," Zhi Lan insisted, stepping over the raised threshold. "I told you I was running an errand."

He smiled at her, as if he were not surprised by this. "Come here, then. Tell me what you think."

She approached his table, her eyes falling on the painting he was working on. "Oh!"

Upon the silk was a near replica of his original painting of Shui Jin Mountain, from the sloping rocks to the frothy white waterfall.

"You've done it," Zhi Lan said in a hushed voice. She knelt across from him. "But...I thought it was impossible!"

"Anything is possible when one's life is on the line," Master Dan said, his eyes sparkling. It sounded like a jest.

Zhi Lan ducked her head. Suddenly, she felt extremely foolish. "Magistrate Bu didn't give you a hard time when I was gone, did he?"

"Ah, him? His tantrum is ongoing, but nothing terrible has befallen me. I can handle a few glares and curses," her master said. "He did ask where *you* were, though. I told him you were running errands for me. I presume that's only half true?"

Zhi Lan fidgeted. Heat blazed her cheeks. The ruined painting in her hand felt heavy and useless.

Master Dan waited patiently for her to say more.

Zhi Lan should've known that Master Dan would've been fine on his own. She hadn't considered the possibility that Magistrate Bu's threat was merely a passing comment made in anger. He was the most powerful man Zhi Lan had ever met in her life. How was she supposed to know whether he meant his threats or not?

All this time, she could have very well stayed and helped Master Dan with his painting instead of going on a wild goose chase with Shao Qing. She had been convinced that following the thief was the swiftest option to set things right.

She had grossly overreacted.

"I've done something very stupid," Zhi Lan confessed.

"Did you buy the wrong paint?" Master Dan asked mildly.

She buried her face into her hands, wondering if she was about to scandalize her poor master.

"I...I was trying to get your painting back," Zhi Lan said. "From the thief who stole it."

With a deep breath, she told him of Shao Qing coming to her room, of the deal she struck with him, and the trail they had followed to Yun City to steal back the painting. Master Dan listened to all of this with serene silence, raising his brows every now and then.

"We nearly got caught. Magistrate Li saw my face. I'm afraid we can no longer travel there," she said sheepishly.

Master Dan shook his head. "You didn't have to go to such lengths for me, child."

Zhi Lan hung her head. "My reasons were somewhat self-ish. Everything was going so well for us. For me. I didn't want to lose this opportunity."

"That's understandable."

"After Magistrate Bu's banquet—"

"You mean his temper tantrum."

Zhi Lan let out a startled laugh. "Well yes, after that. What he said about letting you hang..." She shuddered. "You seemed hopeless that night. I was certain you wouldn't be able to do the replica. In any case...I got the original back." She opened the sodden painting in her arms, rolling it out before Master Dan. It had only gotten worse during the journey. The silk was badly buckled. Only vague blotches of color remained. Some of the ink had transferred onto the back of the brocade.

Master Dan sighed. They had a moment of mournful silence for the masterpiece that had been.

"You always said that everything we paint should have a deeper meaning," Zhi Lan said, crossing her arms and laying her head on the table. She was dreadfully tired. "Repainting this must've been difficult for you."

Her master patted her arm. "I'm afraid my ideologies have held me back, child. This was more difficult for me than it ought to have been. And it seems I gave you such a fright that you resorted to desperate measures." He tapped the back of his brush to his current work in progress. "Perhaps there is less soul in this replica than the original, but it functions as it should. In any case, others may assign their own meaning upon seeing it. This painting possesses deeper meaning regardless of whether I intended it or not. I am satisfied with that. Are you, Zhi Lan?"

Zhi Lan nodded slowly. "May I ask you something, Master Dan?"

"Of course."

"What you said about people assigning deeper meaning to art...do you think that can apply to a person as well?"

Master Dan stroked his beard. "I believe so."

"Is it possible to think better of someone, to think they are good and kind, even if they claim they don't have the capacity for it?"

"How you view a person depends on how you view the world. If you see the world as good and kind, it's only natural you will find those qualities in the people you meet."

Zhi Lan lifted her head, thinking this over. What if she had deluded herself about the kind of person Shao Qing was? He was like a blank piece of paper, and she had merely drawn a picture right over him. She wanted to believe he was a good man in need of saving. But she was always rushing into things, trusting her gut and reacting accordingly. She had overreacted with Magistrate Bu's threat. Who knew whether her instincts about Shao Qing were correct, or if she were merely assigning deeper meaning to him when there was none?

She had never been so unsure in her life.

"Are you thinking about your thief?" Master Dan said, raising his eyebrows.

Zhi Lan made a face. "He is not *my* thief. But yes, I was. There is something unusual about him."

Quickly, she told Master Dan of Shao Qing's soulless condition, his demonic bargain, and the promise she had made to find his soul. She also told him of the small, kind things she had noticed about him. She didn't tell him the specifics of Shao Qing's sister—that part was not for her to share.

"He's honorable in spite of being soulless," Zhi Lan admitted. "He kept his word to me. And I...I suppose I just want to help."

"From what you told me, I think his soul is worth finding," Master Dan said kindly. "You are a good girl, Zhi Lan. This Shao Qing is lucky to have you."

She rolled her eyes at this, knowing her master was openly teasing her now. Then, she sat up, suddenly alert. "Do you remember that dragon painting in Magistrate Bu's collection?"

THE NEXT MORNING, MAGISTRATE BU summoned them to the parlor.

Master Dan and Zhi Lan went immediately after breakfast, bearing the finished replica of Shui Jin Mountain. Zhi Lan was as nervous as she had been three days ago when she had first stepped foot in the magistrate's manor—though this time, it was for an entirely different reason.

Just as they passed the threshold of the parlor, Zhi Lan caught a glimpse of the door that led to Magistrate Bu's art collection. Her heart beat a little faster when she thought of what could possibly be inside. She'd have to look into it later.

And maybe in the afternoon, she'd make some excuse to go out and find Shao Qing.

"Your lordship," Master Dan said, bowing low.

Zhi Lan scrambled to do the same.

Magistrate Bu was reclined on a cushioned chair, watching a maid pour him tea. "Ah, Li Chen. I see your little apprentice is back."

Zhi Lan lowered her head, keeping her gaze downcast.

"I apologize for her sudden absence," Master Dan said. "Zhi Lan was fetching paint for me. I'm very particular about the type I get."

Magistrate Bu was silent as he swirled his tea. "You have what I asked for?"

Master Dan stepped forward and offered the replica scroll to him. The magistrate took it and unfurled it slowly, his narrowed eyes assessing the picture as it revealed itself.

"Very good," Magistrate Bu said at last. He looked up, smiling. "Now all that is left is to find the thief who stole from me. I hope to have this matter solved today."

Zhi Lan blinked. A part of her had thought he would let it go once he got the replicated painting in his hands. But she realized how naive that was. It wasn't about the painting at all. It was about the magistrate's pride. His position. He needed to make an example of those who stole from him.

"Who accompanied you during your errand, Miss Zhi Lan?" Magistrate Bu said, suddenly addressing her.

She grew cold. "No one, my lord."

"No one? That's unusual, for a young woman."

"I'm from a farming village. Very few of us need accompaniment on errands."

Magistrate Bu sipped his tea. "According to my guards, you left with a male servant of mine."

Zhi Lan wanted to kick herself. Shao Qing hadn't gone unnoticed after all.

"Forgive me, your lordship," Master Dan cut in. "My student is merely confused. She had not much rest and—"

Magistrate Bu held up a hand. "Leave us for a moment, Li Chen. I wish to speak with your student alone."

Master Dan frowned, throwing Zhi Lan a concerned look. She nodded ever so slightly, telling him that she'd be fine. It was a bold faced lie—she was panicking. But she didn't want her master involved in whatever this was.

Master Dan bowed and exited the parlor, leaving Zhi Lan and the magistrate alone. She realized that the servants had inconspicuously left in the middle of the meeting. Every muscle in her body tensed.

"Straighten up, my dear. No one likes a wilting flower."

Stiffly, Zhi Lan straightened. She kept her gaze on the floor.

Magistrate Bu stood from his seat, his silk robe rustling as he walked in a slow circle around her.

Her breathing grew shallow as his pristine shoes stopped inches before hers.

"You are a very tempting thing, you know?" Magistrate Bu purred. He reached out, tugging a strand of hair behind her ear.

Zhi Lan flinched away. The magistrate withdrew, chuckling.

She clenched her jaw, equal parts dismayed and terrified. Magistrate Bu was exactly who Zhi Lan suspected he was from the beginning—a sick bastard who liked having women at his mercy.

In her village, taking advantage of girls was condemned. Men like him were shamed or driven out. But Zhu City wasn't the village. She recalled what Yao and Shao Qing had said: The ones in charge of justice were often the source of injustice.

They were right.

"Two days ago you left my home with a man who was not in my employ, and then you came back without him. Who was he?" Magistrate Bu asked. He was too close. Close enough that Zhi Lan could count the silken stitches that made up the bamboo embroidered on his robe.

"You must be mistaken, my lord," Zhi Lan said, sticking to her story. Her palms grew clammy. "I left alone."

"Did you know lying to a magistrate is a punishable offense?" Magistrate Bu said in a low, soft voice, his sour breath washing over her face. "Fifty strikes of a bamboo rod and five years of hard labor."

Zhi Lan trembled in spite of herself.

He closed a heavy hand around her shoulder and squeezed, his hard fingers digging into her flesh. "A beauty like you should never suffer such a fate," he crooned. "You deserve to be dripping in gold and jade, sleeping in silk sheets. I can give you that. Only if you tell me who you are protecting. Whatever he can give you, I can give you ten thousand times over."

She was reminded of the nobleman who had propositioned her all those years ago, of his leering face, his pretty promises, and unbidden touches.

Zhi Lan wished to scream, to withdraw and condemn him for such advances. But this man was the magistrate of the city. She was merely a farm girl at his mercy.

To protect herself in one way was to endanger herself in another.

Once again, Zhi Lan was faced with a smart choice and a principled choice. She could save herself and Master Dan by accepting the magistrate's offer. She'd be gaining a lavish future. Her family would benefit.

Or she could refuse him and suffer the consequences. She knew herself too well for the decision to be difficult.

"I don't like gold or jade, my lord," Zhi Lan said quietly. She met the magistrate's eyes, hoping he saw her defiance and not her fear. "As for silk? I only wish for the kind to paint on."

Magistrate Bu's face hardened, his lips drawing back in a snarl. His hold on Zhi Lan tightened, his thumb digging into her collarbone with bruising force. "I'll teach you a lesson, you—"

"Husband." A soft yet commanding voice interrupted his threat. "You were not at breakfast."

Lady Bu swept in, dressed in regal blue, her face serene. Her steps were purposeful as she stopped beside Zhi Lan and greeted Magistrate Bu with a bow.

"Wife," the magistrate growled, letting go of Zhi Lan's shoulder. She sucked in a uneven breath.

Lady Bu straightened. The lady stood nearly a full head taller than Zhi Lan, meeting the magistrate eye to eye. "I'm afraid I must take Miss Nong from you. She has agreed to accompany me out for the day."

He sneered. "Get some maidservant or other. I'm talking to her."

"I am visiting my father today," Lady Bu said. The magistrate stiffened at this. "I have told him of the painters we've acquired recently. He wants to meet them."

Magistrate Bu threw down his arms, his sleeves snapping behind him. With a poisonous glare, he said, "Give Magistrate Li my regards."

Lady Bu and Zhi Lan walked out of the parlor in silence.

Tears blurred Zhi Lan's vision and she swiped them away. She felt angry and helpless and terrified all at once.

"You were very brave," Lady Bu finally said, her voice gentler now that she was no longer speaking to her husband.

"I-I don't know what you're talking about, my lady," Zhi Lan stammered. It wouldn't be polite to speak of such things out loud.

Lady Bu stopped beside a rock sculpture, regarding her silently. Zhi Lan wondered if the lady blamed her for seducing her husband. But her next words were not about the magistrate at all.

"Tell me about the young man you left with that morning. Who is he really?"

Zhi Lan looked up, her mouth growing dry. She couldn't be sure whether she could fully trust Lady Bu. What if she were trying to get information from her on the magistrate's behalf?

"I will not tell my husband," the lady said, sensing Zhi Lan's hesitation. "I have no wish to help him. I'm only... curious."

Lady Bu's eyes were pleading, though Zhi Lan couldn't imagine why. Still, there was an earnestness to her face and she had been nothing but kind so far.

"He's...not a servant," Zhi Lan admitted. She still thought it unwise to admit that Shao Qing was the thief the magistrate was looking for.

Lady Bu didn't seem to mind this. "What is his name?"

"Shao Qing, my lady."

"Do you know of his family?" she asked.

"He's an orphan."

Lady Bu furrowed her brows. "Did his parents pass?"

"I don't know, my lady. He says he was found behind a pleasure house."

"In this city?"

Zhi Lan nodded uncertainly, wondering why Lady Bu was so interested in Shao Qing's background.

"Thank you for telling me." She rested her hand on Zhi Lan's shoulder, her touch gentle where the magistrate's had been punishing. "Are you in pain?"

Zhi Lan shook her head. There was some pain, but it was nothing compared to what she thought was going to happen. She felt like crying again. "How do you stand him?" she hazarded to ask. "Does he hurt you like this?"

Lady Bu smiled mirthlessly. "He won't touch me unless I permit it. I am not powerless. I have my family behind me. But you..."

Zhi Lan didn't need to hear the rest. She knew her background was humble and that she was an easy target for someone like the magistrate. Meanwhile, Lady Bu was the daughter of someone of equal standing as Magistrate Bu. She blinked, suddenly nervous.

"You don't truly mean to bring me to Magistrate Li, do you, my lady?" Zhi Lan asked.

Lady Bu's smile softened. "Not if you wish it. But you ought to follow me out in any case. It's best to avoid my husband when he is angry."

They made it out the gate. A carriage was waiting outside, and Lady Bu ascended it, drawing the window curtain aside to peer out at Zhi Lan.

"Do you have somewhere to go?" the lady asked. "Let me drop you off."

Zhi Lan clasped her hands and bowed. "Thank you, Lady Bu. I will be fine on my own."

"Then the best of luck to you, child."

The lady and her carriage clip clopped down the road in the direction of the city gate. Zhi Lan sighed, shielding her eyes from the sun.

A clash of a bell sounded near the *yamen*, but Zhi Lan was too far away to investigate. Since she was out, she might as well run her errand early. She had planned to go back to Yao and An Qin and ask them about Shao Qing's whereabouts. It was too bad she hadn't had the chance to look into the magistrate's art room or speak to Master Dan, but there was no turning back now.

Poor Master Dan. She was proving to be an unwieldy student to him.

Zhi Lan followed the winding path Shao Qing had first taken her through. She even managed to make it over the boarded up door in the alleyway without help. After scaling walls and running along roofs, a climb over a door wasn't so bad.

As she straightened her skirts, someone tugged on her sleeve.

It was the little street urchin who had attempted to rob her a few days before. She looked cleaner now, her small face wiped clean of dirt and her tattered robe replaced by a sturdy green one that looked a tad too big for her.

"I have nothing to steal," Zhi Lan said crossly, shaking her sleeve free.

"I came to say thank you for the money, miss," the girl said. "The young master who gave it to me said it was yours."

Zhi Lan tilted her head at this. "When did he tell you that?"

"Last night. I saw him and wondered if he had more to give me," the urchin said.

Her lips tugged up. "And did he?"

"He told me to go to the herbalist shop for a job. I'm respectable now," the urchin said, patting her puny chest.

If Zhi Lan had any lingering doubts, they eased slightly. It appeared that Shao Qing had a heart after all. Zhi Lan squatted so she was level with the little urchin. "I'm looking for this young master," she said. "Have you seen him today?"

To her relief, the urchin nodded. "He went to the place where adults go."

Zhi Lan frowned at this. "Where's that?"

The urchin merely took her sleeve again and led Zhi Lan down the street. After a few turns, they stopped in front of a three-story building.

"There," the urchin said.

Zhi Lan swallowed, her gaze sweeping over the gaudy red banners and perfumed women giggling near the windows.

Skies. She couldn't believe she was about to walk into a pleasure house for some stinky thief.

15

S HAO QING HADN'T TAKEN A bath in over a month.
Just as dawn cracked, he entered the public bathhouse. A few pools of steaming water dotted the
room, soaking the air in fog. The bathhouse owner gave him a
towel and a cake of soap before showing him down to a pool
situated in a far corner.

As it was early in the day, the water was still fresh. Shao
Qing stripped off and submerged himself. The heat eased his
muscles. After sniffing his underarms, he realized that he did,
in fact, stink. He wondered why he hadn't noticed before.

He put the soap to good use.

When he finished scrubbing himself, Shao Qing laid his
head back, watching the swirls of steam rise from his bath-
water. It was an insignificant thing, something he wouldn't
have paid any mind to three days ago. Now, he observed the
water vapors dance and dissolve into nothingness, wondering
how Zhi Lan with her artist's eye would interpret something
so inconsequential. What would it be like to view the world

through her eyes? How vivid colors and objects would be. He didn't even have the capacity to imagine it.

Shao Qing didn't realize how long he had been there until more patrons entered the bathhouse. The morning was growing late.

"Did you hear? Magistrate Bu caught the thief he was hunting for!" a man exclaimed. "He turned himself in not ten minutes ago. Struck the bell himself!"

"Good riddance! Now he can finally listen to his petitioners."

"We may have to wait until tomorrow. Apparently his lordship is sentencing the man today."

"Do you think there will be a public beheading?"

"I hope not. It'll hold up the traffic."

Shao Qing considered this. A thief was caught, yet it wasn't him. Had it been someone in Yao's group?

His musings were answered when sometime later, Yao himself bustled through the front doors of the bathhouse along with half the gang. They approached just as Shao Qing was getting out of the pool.

"Why this sudden obsession with hygiene, Brother Qing?" Wei asked, sitting himself noisily on the damp bench beside him.

Nan You gave a low whistle as his gaze dropped. "Nice dragon, Brother Qing. Not so little after all, huh?"

Shao Qing covered himself with his towel.

Yao, Xuan Bo, and Nan You joined Wei on the bench.

"You owe us a story, eh?" Xuan Bo leaned forward and clasped his hands on his knees. "Tell us how the heist with your girl went."

It appeared that Yao had told everyone about Shao Qing's excursion to Magistrate Li's manor. They were all curious about how it had gone, and about his new "lady friend".

Shao Qing didn't indulge them. He pulled on his clothes. "I heard Magistrate Bu caught his thief. Allegedly he turned himself in."

This seemed to surprise them all.

"Really?" Wei whispered, his eyes wide. "It isn't one of us, as far as I know. It might be a trick to let our guard down."

"Or his lordship truly means to wash his hands of it. Why not grab any old fellow and pin the blame on him? It's a classic ploy for any magistrate to avoid a demerit and save face. It'll appear like a just, swift sentencing," Yao said.

They all sat there, contemplating.

Shao Qing wondered if the sudden whirlwind of events of the last few days had finally come to an end. Magistrate Bu was no longer pursuing him. Zhi Lan had her painting back. Well, her *ruined* painting. He wondered if she was alright. Would she find him again, like she said? Or was she in trouble and trapped in the magistrate's manor?

The thought bothered him. It would be idiotic to go back to check. Yet...

Nan You thumped Shao Qing's back. "Brothers, let's go to The Peony Pagoda!"

"But it's so early," Wei said, appalled.

Nan You smoothed a hand over his goatee. "Perhaps you're too young to know, little Wei, but a man can enjoy wine and women at any hour of the day."

"Well, I suppose it *is* time for breakfast. Their dishes are not bad," Yao conceded. "What do you say, Brother Qing?"

Shao Qing nodded. He had nowhere else to go, anyhow.

"Wei, you had better stay behind," Yao said. "You're too young for these vices."

Wei frowned and sulked, but eventually left.

Shao Qing followed the rest of the men to the place of his alleged birth.

Most men drank to numb themselves. Shao Qing drank to feel something.

It didn't signify that the only thing he felt was ill and hot in the face, but it was better than the odd, dull ache in his chest. Some sort of forlorn longing, as if he wished to relive last night, when Zhi Lan had ranted at him—not to argue over some principle they disagreed on—but for his well-being. When had anyone ever done that?

Yao sat across from Shao Qing at a small square table. The other two were seated in an adjacent chamber, separated by beaded curtains behind which several courtesans cooed and giggled over them. Yao was ever loyal to his wife, but he frequented the pleasure house to chug their wine, which he claimed was one of the best in the city. Shao Qing couldn't taste the difference.

"So. How *did* it go?" Yao asked in a low voice.

"It was successful, but unsuccessful," Shao Qing said.

Yao barked a laugh. "Two days with a scholar painter and you're already speaking in riddles. So what, you got the painting but lost the girl? Was the young miss scared off by your condition?"

"My...condition?"

"You're unnatural. Cursed."

Shao Qing looked up. "You knew?"

"I know the look of those demon-touched," Yao said, tapping his eye. "You have it all over you."

"Why take me in then?"

"A good thief is a good thief. I don't discriminate. And you *did* save my life," he said with a shrug. "Although all those reckless behaviors you've been engaging in have been getting on my last nerve. Tell me. What happened to you?"

Shao Qing swallowed his nausea. The pink drapery and gaudy furniture of the pleasure house swam in his vision. In a low voice, he gave an abbreviated account of his bargain with the bamboo demon. Zhi Lan was the first person he'd told his story to in its entirety. She might be the last.

"You exchanged your soul to become fearless?" Yao asked incredulously. "How are you still alive?"

"It took my soul, not my life."

"The only reason any of us are alive is because we fear death. Fear protects us. Only dead fools are fearless."

"I did not think it was an unreasonable exchange," Shao Qing said.

Yao shook his head at this. "Hm. So she left, then? I don't see any woman tolerating you in this state."

Shao Qing took another swig of wine, even as his throat burned in protest. "She wants to help me find my soul."

Yao's eyes nearly popped out of its sockets. "Really?"

"I don't know if I want it back."

"Of course you don't want it back, you don't even have the capacity to care!" Yao exclaimed. "She is right, however.

It is not a matter of want, but need. A body is meant to have a soul, Brother Qing. It is the natural order of things." He patted his stomach, which let out a loud gurgle. "Speaking of nature, I need to find a privy."

Yao stood up and disappeared through a curtain, shooing off the courtesans that scampered after him.

Shao Qing returned to his drink, considering what Yao had said. He supposed it was true, but he still couldn't bring himself to regret the bargain. He wondered if that was how things were going to be from now on. An ocean of passivity, with nothing and no one to break up the endless waters.

A courtesan in white approached the table. Shao Qing waved a dismissive hand.

"I don't need your services."

He was suddenly assaulted by a hard poke on the side of his head. He looked up, disoriented. When his vision refocused, he saw Zhi Lan standing over him with her hands on her hips.

"I didn't know you worked here," he slurred. "Or have you come to enjoy the women with me?" He was goading a reaction out of her, and was satisfied when she scowled.

She had come for him, like she said.

"You don't enjoy anything, Shao Qing." Zhi Lan sat beside him in a huff, more irate than usual. Her robe was crinkled at the shoulder, her collar slightly askew. A purplish bruise peeked out from above her collarbone.

Without thinking, Shao Qing grazed his fingertips over it. She startled, but didn't move away. Her skin was soft like a flower petal. He would've dared to explore further if Zhi Lan didn't finally shake him off.

"Just so you know, I *don't* work here," she said gruffly, straightening her robe.

"Is that bruise recent?"

"I'm alive, that's all that matters."

Shao Qing drank her in, remembering what she had told him last night. It seemed almost...unreal that she cared so much.

Zhi Lan looked around, raising her brows at the courtesans giggling and serving their patrons. "Why are you here so early? It's broad daylight!"

Shao Qing took another swig of his wine. "There's no place more fitting for me to be. I was born here. Maybe I'll die here too."

Zhi Lan grabbed the jar of wine from him, sloshing some on herself. She didn't seem to notice. "Magistrate Bu is looking for a thief—well, he's looking for you. You're not safe here."

"Magistrate Bu has already found his thief. The whole city knows."

A crease appeared between her eyebrows. "What? That can't be. He was intent on finding you just this morning."

Shao Qing shook his head, but the action only made the room spin. "He must have found someone to take my place. I told you. He only cares to save face." He squeezed his eyes shut and pressed his fingers to his temple.

"Does this place serve sober-up soup?" Zhi Lan asked. Her voice sounded far away.

"Yes, miss!"

"Get me a bowl, please."

When Shao Qing opened his eyes, a courtesan came back with a bowl. Zhi Lan thanked her and set the bowl in front of him.

Noodles floated in clear broth with sliced beef and a boiled egg. Zhi Lan thrust a pair of chopsticks and a soup spoon into his hands.

"Eat. Once you're feeling better we can talk." She looked concerned. Something about that was comforting.

Shao Qing obeyed. The soup didn't taste like anything, but it was hot and soothed his throat. He was slightly less nauseated when he finished. "What do you have to say to me?" he finally said.

Her face was serious. "I think I've found your soul, Shao Qing. It's been right under our noses. Magistrate Bu has it."

Shao Qing sat very still. "How do you know it's mine?"

Zhi Lan bit her lower lip. "I don't. But there's a chance it might be." She looked at him hesitantly. "Are you willing to follow me and find out?"

This was different from her forceful speech the other night. Something had shaken her resolve, and Shao Qing didn't know what.

"I'll follow you anywhere." He felt that they were the truest words he had ever spoken. Zhi Lan was like a rock in the middle of his ocean. He had never felt more awake than in her presence.

Zhi Lan's cheeks turned pink. "Oh." She tilted her head and leaned toward him as she inhaled, her lashes fluttering. "Did you...bathe?"

Shao Qing held his breath. The air around his neck felt hot. Zhi Lan was close enough that he could lift her chin and kiss her if he wanted to. The errant thought startled him.

Did he want to?

"What's this, Brother Qing? A scholar girl? Are they catering to all sorts of tastes now?" Nan You came noisily through the beaded curtain, then stopped before them. He whistled. "Not bad."

Zhi Lan stood suddenly, rattling the table. There was a feral glint in her eye. "I do *not* work here so cease gawping at me unless you want your eyes gouged out!"

Nan You raised his hands in surrender. "Apologies, miss."

Zhi Lan brushed off her robes in disgust. "Men."

Shao Qing stood too. "I'm leaving, Nan You. Tell Yao when he comes back."

They left a sheepish Nan You behind them as they started for the stairs.

16

ZHI LAN REENTERED MAGISTRATE BU'S manor through the front gates, her heart at her throat.

Just outside, Shao Qing was climbing up the west wall. She kept her gaze lowered, not wanting to give away his position.

From the corner of her eye Zhi Lan saw a dark figure emerge over the roof.

At that moment, a servant girl walked past the courtyard, a basket of laundry tucked under her arm.

Zhi Lan ran to her side. "Excuse me!"

The servant girl looked at Zhi Lan expectantly. Shao Qing was making his way down, dangling from the lip of the roof several feet above the ground. His landing wouldn't be a quiet one.

"Where has Magistrate Bu gone?" Zhi Lan asked quickly.

"His lordship is preparing for the tribunal, miss. Shall I let him know you're looking for him?" the servant girl inquired.

"Oh, no! Not at all! Please, go on."

The servant girl nodded and continued down her path.

Shao Qing landed on the west veranda with a heavy thump.

Zhi Lan coughed violently into her sleeve. The servant girl turned, her face puzzled.

"Apologies. Something in my throat," Zhi Lan wheezed.

Shao Qing slipped into her room. The servant girl bobbed her head and disappeared into the east wing.

With a sigh, Zhi Lan quickly entered her room after him.

To her surprise, Master Dan was sitting at her desk, looking curiously at Shao Qing.

"There's a stranger in your room, Zhi Lan," Master Dan said after a beat of silence.

She bowed sheepishly. It seemed that Shao Qing hadn't bothered to introduce himself. She made the introductions now.

"Ah. I've heard a great deal about you, young man," Master Dan said once it was done.

Shao Qing bowed.

"Master, I meant to tell you that I went out, but I didn't get the chance," Zhi Lan said quickly.

Master Dan tilted his head in concern. "Never mind that. What did Magistrate Bu wish to speak to you about?"

Zhi Lan shuddered when she recalled the meeting. It was a lucky thing Lady Bu had come to her rescue. "Nothing," she said, not wishing to share this with him. It was too soon and too humiliating.

"Did the magistrate give you that bruise?" Shao Qing asked from his corner.

Master Dan furrowed his brow at this. "Bruise? He laid his hands on you?"

Zhi Lan felt like shrinking. "I'd rather not speak of this, Master Dan."

This seemed to tell him all he wished to know. "Zhi Lan. Don't be ashamed," Master Dan said gently. "If anyone should feel shame, it should be the magistrate. And me. You are under my care. I've done you a disservice by putting you at the mercy of a dishonorable man."

Tears suddenly stung Zhi Lan's eyes. She had thought that she had composed herself already, but evidently not. Her vision blurred, rendering the image of her dear master to a white blob. "I-I…"

"There, there child. Don't cry," he said, standing to pat her hand. "I think it's time that we leave this place."

"Leave?" Zhi Lan sniffed and wiped her eyes. "But he's our patron!"

"He's a brute and an immoral man," Master Dan said with a firm shake of his head. "I had suspected, but it's never been clearer now. I daresay you've suffered much on my behalf. I won't allow it to go on any longer." His gaze softened. "This is why I wanted you to go home, child. This life isn't safe for you like it is safe for me."

"But Master—"

"No one harms my student," Master Dan said firmly. "I will speak to his lordship before the day is done."

Zhi Lan stayed silent, not wishing to be the cause of Master Dan making such a drastic decision. She had offended Magistrate Bu that morning. If anything, she should be the one to leave. Master Dan could still benefit from his patronage. Still, Zhi Lan knew her master was not the sort of man who only cared for his own gain. She was touched by his concern for her and grateful for his gentility. There were not many men like him.

"Perhaps we can talk about this later," Zhi Lan said reluctantly. "But first, I brought Shao Qing here because..."

Master Dan nodded. "Ah, yes. I remember." He turned to Shao Qing. "May you find your soul, young man."

Shao Qing bowed again. "Thank you, sir."

After waiting for the servants to pass, the two of them slipped quickly into the art room.

Zhi Lan closed the door behind her softly. "It's in here." She was still discomfited from earlier, but forced herself to calm. It wouldn't do to get distracted now. She had brought a thief into the magistrate's manor, and she needed a clear mind to get him out without notice.

The room was as she had seen it last, a cluttered collection of precious treasures, each one stacked on top of another.

Shao Qing gave a low whistle. "Impressive."

They passed the crowded walls of paintings and calligraphy. Zhi Lan mourned that none of them would ever be appreciated as they should. It was clear now that Magistrate Bu did not admire art—not truly. It was only a symbol of status and wealth to him. What a waste for such a collection to belong to such a man.

Zhi Lan recalled that the magistrate's steward had placed the painting on a circular shelf in the far left corner of the room. She went there now, pulling Shao Qing with her, then stopped abruptly.

It had also been the corner full of bawdy artwork.

Zhi Lan's cheeks heated when her eyes flew over the silk screen that depicted the couple underneath the willow tree. What had it been called?

Scenery of the Spring Palace.

Shao Qing raised an eyebrow at the screen. "If this is what you wanted to show me, we could have stayed at the pleasure house."

"This is *not* what I wanted to show you," Zhi Lan whispered harshly. She felt warm all over. She turned to the shelf in front of her, rummaging through the many scrolls, bronze sculptures, and jade statuettes. "Help me look, will you?"

He obliged. They opened each scroll, revealing paintings of tigers and forests, bold calligraphy and classic poems. Zhi Lan didn't bother being neat when she put the scrolls away. She had a feeling the magistrate did not frequent his hoard as often as he had people think.

Shao Qing's hand closed around a scroll at the very bottom shelf. He stilled.

Zhi Lan knelt on the floor beside him, her eyes wide. "Do you feel something?"

"I think so," he said, his voice hoarse. It was the most emotion Zhi Lan had ever heard from him.

"Let's have a look, then."

Shao Qing withdrew the scroll, his hand shaking as he undid the ties. The painting unfurled.

It was just as Zhi Lan remembered. The dragon was rendered with loose brushstrokes, its body curved like a winding river between wispy clouds, its mane gold and its horns a sapphire blue. Now Zhi Lan knew why it looked so life-like. When Shao Qing brushed his hands over the paper, the painting rippled, and suddenly it was moving—*actually* moving.

Zhi Lan gaped. The dragon reared up and weaved over the page, exploring one corner, then the next. Its tail flicked through the clouds, splitting them into smaller puffs of white. It reared and clawed at them like it wanted to tear its way out of the paper, though some invisible barrier stopped it. It was the most stunning piece of art Zhi Lan had ever set her eyes on.

"It can't leave," Shao Qing said. If he was disappointed, Zhi Lan couldn't tell. They crouched over it, silent.

She had half-expected the dragon to jump out and return to its owner in some way—though she wasn't sure. This was her first run in with anything remotely supernatural.

Shao Qing made a move to stand, but Zhi Lan pulled him back down.

"We're not leaving until we figure this out," she insisted.

He only shrugged.

Zhi Lan squinted at the thief, then at the dragon. Shao Qing stared back with his beige, blank eyes.

The dragon's eyes were also blank. Two empty circles the color of parchment.

"That's it!"

Zhi Lan fumbled for the pouch at her belt. She never went anywhere without her painting supplies. Having a brush and ink on hand was very convenient when inspiration struck.

"What is it?" Shao Qing asked, watching her unload a miniature inkstone and ink stick, a brush, and a vial of water.

"Just wait." Zhi Lan dribbled water into the inkstone and ground it quickly with her inkstick. It was Master Dan's cinnabar brown that she had purchased in Yun City. She'd forgotten to give it to him last night.

"Are you going to vandalize my soul?" Shao Qing said when she dipped her brush into the ink and hovered it over the scroll. He splayed his hand over the dragon.

"I'll do nothing of the sort!" Zhi Lan had never vandalized anything in her life, much less a piece of art she admired. "Don't you trust me?"

"I've known you for three days."

"Yet you'll follow me anywhere," Zhi Lan said, echoing his words to her earlier. She meant it to be a teasing comment, and she was so used to Shao Qing not reacting that it shocked her when his ears grew red. He slowly removed his hand.

She felt vindicated by this, knowing in her gut that what she was about to do was the right thing.

The dragon seemed curious, following the tip of Zhi Lan's brush with its nose.

Slowly, with a steady hand that would make Master Dan proud, Zhi Lan dotted the pigment on the dragon's right eye. Then, the left.

The dragon glowed, illuminating their surroundings in golden light. It reared from its page with a silent roar. Its body, now suspended in the air, was made up of wisps of gold lines. Some of them bled toward Shao Qing and tethered to him like shimmering fibers, as if revealing what had been there all along—the pieces of his soul that still clung to him.

Zhi Lan held her breath.

In a swift, arcing motion, the dragon hurtled toward her. Zhi Lan shrieked.

It danced around her in a joyous manner, its tail flicking the ends of her hair and curling around her shoulders. A puff of cool air brushed her cheek as the dragon nuzzled her ear. A ghostly caress. It was a playful soul, she realized.

Shao Qing's face twisted into an unreadable expression as he watched the dragon nestle on her shoulders.

"Why is it on me?" Zhi Lan asked, appalled. She wanted to remove it, but the dragon was like a heavy mist—present yet insubstantial. She was sure her fingers would pass right through it. And besides, touching Shao Qing's *soul* felt a little strange. "Doesn't it recognize you?"

Shao Qing scoffed.

The dragon scoffed right back.

"Maybe it's mad at you for giving it away." Zhi Lan felt the dragon's whiskers tickle her cheek.

"I've been fine without it."

"You have not."

Shao Qing seemed to consider this, but made no answer.

"I'm not keeping it," Zhi Lan said crossly. "You might as well take it since we went through all this trouble."

He remained frustratingly silent, seemingly not in the mood to argue. Zhi Lan wasn't either.

"Su Su would want you to have it back," she said quietly.

Shao Qing grazed his hand over his chest where he kept the red pouch. He stared at the dragon for a moment, then, hesitantly, he reached out a finger to touch its miniature horns. The dragon slithered from Zhi Lan's shoulders, following Shao Qing's hand.

Like ink in water, the creature suddenly dissolved into ribbons of gold, spiraling around his finger and arcing over his body. Finally, like a rushing river, it flowed into his chest and disappeared. Shao Qing staggered back with a gasp, stumbling into the wall behind them.

"Are you alright?" Zhi Lan cried. She took his arm. He had knocked down a painting above them. The heavy brocade fell onto his head, depicting a man and no less than three women engaging in illicit pleasures.

Zhi Lan looked heavenward, cursing Magistrate Bu and his perverted tastes. As if she needed *this* on top of everything else! She tossed the painting aside. Shao Qing groaned.

"Shao Qing?" she asked, nervous when he didn't answer.

What if having his soul back made him go mad? Or what if he proved to be a very different person than Zhi Lan assumed him to be? He could very well be a cold-hearted criminal at his core.

Her worries were not appeased when Shao Qing began to shake. It was an uncontrollable convulsing, and he gasped as if he had become possessed by some evil spirit.

Zhi Lan sat back uneasily, but she steeled herself. He had helped her, so she would stay and return the favor no matter what condition he ended up in. Whatever happened, she would make it right.

When Shao Qing finally looked up, Zhi Lan realized that he had been weeping. His nose was red and tears streamed from his eyes.

Eyes that were a deep, soulful brown.

17

SHAO QING COULDN'T THINK. TEARS flowed down his cheeks like hot, uncontrollable rivers. His shoulders racked with sobs, weighed by grief he couldn't recall. His chest constricted, too tight and too full. His eyes burned. He was trembling. He felt sick.

The world was so intense.

Small hands touched his shoulders. Someone offered him a blinding white handkerchief.

When he blinked back the dark spots in his vision, Zhi Lan appeared before him. Her delicately arched brows were furrowed. Memories from the past three days crashed over him like a tidal wave. He relived each conversation anew. Every look. Every touch. Shao Qing stopped breathing, gazing at her with feverish intensity. She was so...so...

"How do you feel?" Her voice was nothing short of musical.

Zhi Lan pressed the back of her hand to his forehead. Her

skin was as soft as silk. Shao Qing didn't remember what silk felt like. But surely it couldn't compare to the girl before him.

"Skies, you're burning up!"

"For you." His tongue felt like cotton in his mouth.

"This is no time for jokes!" Zhi Lan exclaimed. "Let's get you out of here before someone finds us." She began to stand, but Shao Qing cupped the back of her neck, forcing her to sit.

"Stop. You're like a bird. Always about to flit away."

Zhi Lan stared at him as if he had grown a second head. "My goodness," she whispered. "You really are ill."

She said something else, but Shao Qing had stopped listening. He leaned in until her perfectly shaped lips were an inch away.

"I'm going to kiss you."

Vaguely, he recalled that he'd been kissed only once by the courtesan who had attended him. It had been an insistent pressing of lips and tongues, and he hadn't liked it. He had a feeling it was because he hadn't been kissing the right person.

Zhi Lan widened her eyes. He waited for her to protest. Even as the thought of kissing her consumed him, he cared very much whether she was willing or not.

She nodded ever so slightly.

It started first as a soft brush of lips, and Shao Qing was lost. Sensual heat pooled to his core, nearly setting him aflame. He drew her to his chest. Zhi Lan gasped, her lips parting as his hands curved over her waist. He kissed her slowly and deeply. His kissed her until he grew drunk off her lips. He kissed her neck. The back of her ear.

Cool hands cupped his cheeks and kept him from leaning in for more.

Zhi Lan was saying something again.

Black spots appeared in his vision.

Then, nothing.

S HAO QING HAD A NEAR psychotic fit, kissed her in a
most wanton manner, then fainted right onto her lap.
Scoundrel.

Never mind that she rather liked it.

Zhi Lan regarded the unconscious Shao Qing, her mouth
still burning and her breath still short from his kisses. He had
tasted like chrysanthemum wine, heady and aromatic. And
if she wasn't mistaken, he *had* bathed. He smelled like fresh
clothes and some sort of woodsy soap. His hair was slightly
damp beneath her fingers.

She sat very still, considering what just happened. She was
sure he had only been momentarily overtaken by ardor and
she just happened to be the first woman he set his eyes on. It
made sense. Who knew what he had been in the middle of
before she found him in the pleasure house? Having his soul
back probably amplified such desires.

Zhi Lan had to admit that passing curiosity was the reason for her consent. She had never been kissed before, and

Shao Qing *was* a handsome man. But that kiss! It was as if he had been making love to her with nothing but his mouth.

Her face flamed at this thought. She couldn't tell who had taken advantage of whom.

With some effort, Zhi Lan pushed him against the wall again so he was slumped upright. She patted his cheek. "Hey."

He didn't stir. Zhi Lan gingerly held a finger under his nose, relieved when she felt him exhale. He was still alive, at least.

She considered what to do. She could go get Master Dan. But she confessed she didn't want to think about her master after what had just happened. Besides, how was an elderly man and a girl supposed to drag an unconscious thief out of the room without notice?

It wouldn't do. The only way Shao Qing was getting out of this manor was on his own two feet.

Zhi Lan tucked two arms underneath his armpits and strained to stand. She managed to lift him to his knees before hers gave out. Skies, he was heavy!

She looked toward the door uneasily, worried that some-one would come in and see them.

Impatiently, Zhi Lan shook Shao Qing's shoulders. "Wake up."

His eyelids twitched, but did not open.

"I have a headache," he murmured.

"Let's go back to my room," she said, taking his arm. "Can you stand?"

Shao Qing stood very slowly, as if he were an old man with brittle bones. He still didn't open his eyes.

Zhi Lan pulled him forward. Shao Qing stumbled head-long into the circular shelf. It was a decorative piece of furniture that didn't have much heft to it despite being stacked full of scrolls and treasures.

It teetered precariously backward. Zhi Lan gasped, running to the other side to prop it up—but it was too late. The contents of the shelf crashed to the ground in a deafening cacophony.

Exclamations sounded from outside. The door to the art room burst open.

"What is going on here?" Magistrate Bu bellowed, dressed in his official's robe and hat.

Zhi Lan froze.

Shao Qing chose that moment to vomit the contents of his stomach onto *Scenery of the Spring Palace*.

"A TERRIBLE CRIME HAS BEEN committed beneath my roof!" Magistrate Bu cried.

They knelt on the cold stone floor before the magistrate, who was seated behind an elevated desk. His presence loomed over the hall lined with guards standing at attention. Each of them held a long bamboo rod, ranging from heavy to light—a reminder of the inevitable punishment to come. Beside the magistrate's desk stood his secretary, who kept his head bowed as he recorded the proceedings.

Zhi Lan had never been inside the tribunal of a *yamen* before. She had a feeling this would be her last time, for better or for worse.

Shao Qing knelt beside her, looking sick to his stomach. He had still been dry heaving when the guards dragged them into the *yamen*—which only made her more worried for him. She almost wished he was back to his old soulless self.

Magistrate Bu slammed his desk. "Nong Zhi Lan. You have brought a criminal into my home. You have assisted this thief with his crimes against me after I have shown you and your master nothing but generosity. Do you plead guilty?"

She could plead whichever way and it wouldn't matter. Magistrate Bu was the sole prosecutor and judge, and it was within his power to rule however he pleased. But Zhi Lan would say her piece no matter what.

She raised her chin stiffly. "I do not, your lordship. I have not assisted a thief in any crime against you."

She had assisted Shao Qing in a crime against another magistrate. But that was neither here nor there.

Magistrate Bu narrowed his eyes. "Do you deny bringing this vermin into my home today? I have asked my guards. He is the same man you were seen with on the day you left."

Zhi Lan pressed her lips together. This she could not deny, even though she wished to be contrary. Hopelessness crashed over her. She had gotten herself into deep, deep trouble—but she couldn't bring herself to regret anything she had done that led up to this moment.

The magistrate took her silence as admittance.

"Nong Zhi Lan. You are charged with deceiving an official. According to imperial law, you deserve fifty strikes and five years of hard labor," Magistrate Bu said, his eyes glittering dangerously. "Unless you wish to plead guilty and repent for your crimes. I am not an ungenerous man." He looked at her with meaning.

Zhi Lan clenched her jaw. He was offering again. Disgust roiled in her gut.

"Nothing will compel me to share your bed, magistrate," Zhi Lan said, unable to hold this back. She was proud her voice didn't waver. "I will take whatever punishment you deem fit. *Except* that."

Magistrate Bu's face grew beet red.

"Preposterous! I suggested no such thing, you fox spirit!" He pounded his desk and pointed at Shao Qing. "And you. What is your name?"

"Shao Qing," he said hoarsely. He still looked sickly and pale.

"No family name?"

"No, your lordship."

"Unsurprising," the magistrate said with a sneer. "You're the thief who stole from me. Do you plead guilty?"

Shao Qing's breaths were shallow. He looked almost... afraid. Zhi Lan wished she could comfort him.

"I do, your lordship," Shao Qing said, lowering his head.

Zhi Lan started at this. She had not expected him to confess—in fact, she had hoped he would lie and weasel his way out somehow. Had his soul made an honest man out of him?

What rotten luck.

Magistrate Bu smiled smugly. "Thieving from a bureaucrat is a capital offense. You're to hang at dawn."

Zhi Lan couldn't breathe. She looked to Shao Qing, who merely closed his eyes at the sentencing.

This was her fault.

If she hadn't insisted on getting his soul back, he would have never returned to Magistrate Bu's manor and fallen into his clutches. Now Shao Qing was to die—and feel every torturous moment leading up to it.

"I'm sorry," Zhi Lan said, her vision blurring with tears.

Shao Qing met her gaze, his eyes a warm, dark brown. "Don't be."

Magistrate Bu scoffed. "Drag Miss Nong outside for her beating."

Two guards grabbed her arms, pulling her from her knees. Zhi Lan noticed that they held the thickest of the bamboo rods. She felt faint. How was she going to survive fifty strikes of *that*?

Shao Qing suddenly prostrated himself on the ground. "Let me take the beating for her. Miss Nong is of weak constitution. She will not be fit for the rest of her sentence if she suffers this."

"Are you defying me, thief?" Magistrate Bu barked.

"Let me take the beating."

"If you're so eager, you may have fifty strikes of your own. Guards! Take them *both* outside."

Two men grabbed Shao Qing roughly from the ground.

"Shao Qing, are you an idiot?" Zhi Lan cried. His gallantry had only provoked the magistrate and now they both had to suffer.

"I won't be a coward again," Shao Qing said fiercely. His jaw was set in a determined line and Zhi Lan could only look at him, helpless.

Where was the soulless thief without principles when she needed him?

Suddenly, deep resonate peals rang through the tribunal. Zhi Lan felt the vibration to her bones. Someone had struck the bell outside, demanding an audience.

"Not so fast," a familiar voice cried out.

To Zhi Lan's astonishment, Lady Bu walked in with nothing short of a crowd behind her. She spotted a pair of guards, Magistrate Li, an old woman, a dirty stranger bound in ropes, and a middle-aged man who looked extremely familiar.

The man stopped in his tracks, gazing at Shao Qing with shock and unrestrained emotion.

"Wife!" Magistrate Bu barked from his desk. "You go too far! I am in the middle of a ruling."

"This is relevant to your ruling," Lady Bu said. "You yourself have committed a crime against my family. It relates to this young man." She gestured to Shao Qing, still in the guards' grasp. "Let them go and let us talk civilly."

The guards let Zhi Lan and Shao Qing back to the ground. Zhi Lan rubbed her shoulders, wincing.

"What crimes do you speak of?" Magistrate Bu demanded, scowling. "Why have you brought this riff raff?"

"Interesting choice of words," Magistrate Li said, stepping forward. "I would not consider myself *riff raff*."

Magistrate Bu's face darkened at the sight of the older man. "Good riddance. Have you not your own city to rule over?"

"Ruling is for our emperor. I merely enforce justice on his behalf. And you, Magistrate Bu, have caused my family much injustice."

Magistrate Bu sputtered. "What right do you have to make such claims?"

Magistrate Li narrowed his eyes. "Madam Xuan, please step up."

The old woman behind him did so. Her back was bent with age and her coarse gray hair was done up with a plain wooden hairpin. Her face was so wrinkled it looked like a prune.

"Who is this woman?" Magistrate Bu sputtered.

"Don't tell me you don't recognize your own cronies," Magistrate Li said. "Madam, do you wish to remind his lordship?"

"Twenty years ago, I was a nanny. Your lordship gave me nine silver taels," Madam Xuan said.

Magistrate Bu's face grew white, then red. "I recall no such thing!" he bellowed. "What use do I have for a nanny?"

Zhi Lan watched all this in bewilderment, looking from the old woman to Magistrate Li to the middle aged man. She knew why he looked familiar now—he was the spitting image of Shao Qing. She turned to the thief kneeling beside her. Shao Qing looked as lost as she felt.

"You placed me in Magistrate Li's household, to care for Master Wen Jun's newborn child," Madam Xuan said. "I was told to take the child away in the night."

"Ridiculous! A raving madwoman!" Magistrate Bu's face was blotchy. A shiny sheen of sweat coated his forehead.

Madam Xuan continued on, unbothered. "I traveled here to Zhu City and put the baby behind a brothel called The Peony Pagoda. When I told you the deed was done, you rewarded me the silver."

"What was the date?" Magistrate Li said calmly.

"The twenty-eighth day of the ninth month."

Magistrate Li looked to Shao Qing. "What day were you found by the orphanage, young man?"

Shao Qing looked up, his face pale. "The twenty-ninth day of the ninth month."

Magistrate Li withdrew a few papers from his sleeve. "In case you insist on denying this, magistrate, I have personally visited the nearest orphanage from The Peony Pagoda today. Their records indicate that an infant boy by the name of Shao Qing had indeed entered their establishment on that day."

Magistrate Bu's eyes bulged. "So what? Are you claiming kinship with this boy? This *criminal*?"

"I am," a quiet, though commanding voice said. It was the middle-aged man, who Zhi Lan figured was Li Wen Jun, Magistrate Li's son and Shao Qing's birth father. Wen Jun stepped up beside his alleged son.

The resemblance was uncanny—and undeniable. They had the same straight nose, angled jaw, and slanted brows. Only Wen Jun had graying hair at his temples and worry lines around his mouth.

Zhi Lan felt like she was watching an opera unfold. Shao Qing, the long-lost grandson of a magistrate? She felt her head spin, and she swallowed the absurd urge to laugh at the irony.

"And what of it?" Magistrate Bu said, scowling. "Why would this old woman confess such a thing now?"

"I am to pass soon. I wish to free my soul of sins," the old woman croaked. "I have put your silver to good use, my lord, and it has helped my family greatly. But it is black money, and I have no wish to bear this secret any longer."

Magistrate Bu sputtered. "This is entirely unrelated to the case of thievery!"

"Funny my lord would mention that," Lady Bu said. "Your thief seems to have missed his trial."

The pair of guards dragged up the dirty stranger bound in ropes. Zhi Lan didn't recognize him at all—not that she could see much of his face past the dirt and the matted hair. Was this another long-lost relative?

"I found this man detained here last night. But he was let out again this morning to ring the bell and turn himself in," Lady Bu said. "The guards say *he* was the thief who stole from you, and this man admitted to it when I asked him. Imagine my surprise when I heard you had found another thief this morning."

Zhi Lan expected Magistrate Bu to rant and rave again, but he remained silent, his thin lips pressed into a trembling line.

Magistrate Li considered this. "Did you steal a prized painting from Magistrate Bu?" he asked the rope-bound man.

The man whimpered. "N-no. Yes. I...Forgive me!" He kowtowed so violently he almost crashed into the floor.

"A madwoman and now a madman," Magistrate Bu said, his upper lip curling.

"M-my lord, you p-promised that my family will be well taken care of if I confess today," the man stammered. "Does this still hold true?"

"What in heaven's name are you speaking of? Guards, take him away!"

None of the guards moved. The secretary continued to scribble down the proceedings, his brush flying over the page.

The man began to weep, the tears washing the dirt from his cheeks. "Please, my lord, have mercy!"

"Magistrate Bu, perhaps you will be more comfortable here on the floor," Magistrate Li said after a minute of silence broken only by the sobbing man.

Magistrate Bu slammed his hands on his desk. "This is *my* tribunal."

"According to imperial law, the nearest magistrate takes over the ruling if the current magistrate is accused of wrong-doing."

"Who dares accuse me?" Magistrate Bu demanded.

Magistrate Li blinked. "I do. I accuse you of deceit and abuse of power."

"You—"

"Do you disagree with imperial law? Shall we go to the capital city to face the emperor?"

Magistrate Bu snapped his mouth shut.

"I believe you are in my seat," Magistrate Li said evenly.

With a venomous look, Magistrate Bu snapped his sleeves behind him and marched down from his desk. Lady Bu plucked the official's hat off her husband's head and handed it to her father.

Magistrate Bu bristled as Magistrate Li placed the hat on his head and took his seat at the head of the room. Zhi Lan felt the energy change, the pressure in her chest lightening ever so slightly. The sobbing man must have felt the same, as he managed to cease sobbing.

Magistrate Li addressed him. "Did you or did you not steal a prized painting from Magistrate Bu?"

The man kowtowed again. "I did not, your lordship. Magistrate Bu has promised my family wealth if I confessed to stealing from him today."

"Indeed. And why is that?" Magistrate Li said.

"He was unable to find the real thief, so he needed someone to confess before three days were up. I'm only a poor laborer. I can do little for my family, but his lordship offered us riches in exchange for my sentencing," the man said. Then, with a defiant glance at Magistrate Bu, he continued, "It is this humble man's opinion that Magistrate Bu was afraid of losing face and gaining a demerit. He has failed to find thieves and robbers in the past and he's afraid he can no longer keep his office if this goes on."

Magistrate Bu fumed. "You traitorous fool! I'll have your head!" He launched himself at the man and managed a solid kick to his side before a pair of guards restrained him, forcing him to his knees.

"Abuse of power is a capital offense," Magistrate Li said. "Punishable by demotion and imprisonment. Sometimes death."

Magistrate Bu's eyes flashed. He looked like a crazed man. Zhi Lan inched away from him, but the movement only drew his attention. "This changes nothing!" Magistrate Bu spat, his face twisted into a venomous expression. "This girl and that *criminal* you claim as kin have as good as confessed to their crimes. They are thieves and liars! They deserve retribution!"

Zhi Lan flinched as a drop of his spittle landed on her cheek.

"Young miss," Magistrate Li said, his gaze fixating on her. His brows raised slightly when he took in her face. Zhi Lan felt like melting into a puddle. There was no doubt he recognized her. "Who are you, and what do you have to say for yourself?"

Zhi Lan carefully wiped her cheek, then clasped her hands before her in respect before addressing Magistrate Li. "I'm Nong Zhi Lan, my lord. Apprentice to my master, scholar painter Dan Li Chen."

Magistrate Li seemed to recognize Master Dan's name too. His signature stamp had been on the painting of Shui Jin Mountain, which had been in his possession for a full morning.

Slowly, Zhi Lan told him of the stolen painting, Magistrate Bu's threats, her determination to retrieve it, and how Shao Qing had helped her along the way. She kept the locations vague and left out the part about Shao Qing's soul. The case was complicated enough without the supernatural. Zhi Lan knew she was as good as incriminating both of them, but she had a feeling Magistrate Li would be merciful, especially considering that *he* had been the buyer of the stolen painting, and Shao Qing was his grandson.

At the end of her story, Magistrate Li stroked his short beard. "It seems that you were only trying to right a wrong, to steal back what was stolen from you. Though, you have broken into a...*family's* home. You took nothing else but your master's painting, is that correct?"

Zhi Lan nodded slowly, feeling that the magistrate was urging her to agree. It seemed that he was willing to overlook the dragon painting Shao Qing had taken from his study.

"Your intent was to help your master. That dedication is admirable," Magistrate Li said. "Though you still deserve punishment for breaking and entering."

Shao Qing clasped his hands before him. "Your lordship, Zhi Lan cannot be blamed. The fault is mine. I was a bad influence."

Zhi Lan resisted the urge to groan. His newfound gallantry was simultaneously touching and tiresome. Couldn't he see that he was only making things worse?

"I'll get to you later, Li Shao Qing," Magistrate Li said, a sardonic glint in his eye. He addressed Zhi Lan again. "Magistrate Bu's patronage will be terminated. You and your master will no longer receive housing or payment from him. Is that an acceptable punishment for you?"

Magistrate Bu sputtered.

Zhi Lan sagged in relief. "I accept this punishment, my lord," she said, bowing low. Funny. Three days ago this sentencing would've been the death of her.

"Li Shao Qing. You have confessed to thievery," Magistrate Li said.

Shao Qing lowered his head. "Yes, my lord."

"You were raised without principles and have resorted to crime."

Zhi Lan held her breath, wondering if Magistrate Li was going to sentence him to death even if Shao Qing *were* his grandson.

"The fault is on your father, Wen Jun," Magistrate Li said. "Son, you have neglected your parental duty to teach your child the proper way of the world. Do you plead guilty?"

Wen Jun knelt beside Shao Qing. "I do, my lord."

"You will repent by making up for lost time. Take him home and make him into a worthy man."

Wen Jun bowed until his forehead touched the stone floor. "I accept."

Magistrate Bu pounded the tiles. "Unacceptable! I have never heard of such lenient sentencings in my life!"

"You and I have read the same classics, Bu. A child's wrongdoing is a reflection of his parents."

"You are a partial old weasel, Li! I will write your impeachment letter and send it to the capital city. The Ministry of Justice will be hearing about this!"

"My partiality is to my family. Yours is to yourself," Magistrate Li said mildly. "I'll send your impeachment letter as well. We'll see which one of us the ministry thinks is more dastardly."

With that, Magistrate Li concluded the trial.

A crowd was gathering outside the *yamen*, craning their necks over the guards to see what Magistrate Bu had done to his thief.

Zhi Lan could only imagine their surprise when they saw their magistrate dragged along by a pair of guards, kicking and sputtering, followed by a seemingly random collection of strangers.

"Lady Bu," Zhi Lan said, trotting up to her as they made their way back to the manor. "Did you plan all this?"

Magistrate Li, Wen Jun, and Shao Qing trailed some paces behind. The man bound by ropes and the old woman had been allowed to go free.

Lady Bu gave Zhi Lan a mysterious smile. "When I first saw Shao Qing, I had my suspicions. It was only a matter of time before all was revealed."

So that was why Lady Bu had insisted on finding out Shao Qing's name and where he came from. But to imagine that she concocted her plan and gathered all the right people in less than a day!

"I owe you a debt, your ladyship," Zhi Lan said. They entered the manor and passed the courtyard. It felt odd walking into Magistrate Bu's parlor when the master of the house was detained.

Lady Bu had no such scruples, however, and ordered a maidservant to fetch tea. She took her place at the head of the parlor. "You owe me no debt, child. If it weren't for you, my brother would not have found his son."

Zhi Lan looked behind her to see the three men enter the parlor. Shao Qing leaned on his father's arm, still looking sick. Magistrate Li observed them silently as Wen Jun said something too low to hear.

Shao Qing had reunited with his family. She could only imagine the shock he was still feeling, but she was glad he was safe—that they were both safe. She wanted to go and console him, but suddenly she felt like an outsider. After all, everyone else in the room was family. She was just some farm girl.

The maidservant came back with the tea.

Zhi Lan turned back to Lady Bu. "I suppose I'll fetch my master and we'll leave as soon as we can. I don't wish to be a burden to you any longer than necessary."

"You may stay the night. I'm in no rush."

Zhi Lan thanked her for her graciousness. "If I may be so bold to ask, your ladyship, what will happen to Magistrate Bu? Surely this would affect the household and implicate you in some way."

Lady Bu sipped her tea. "I'll have divorce papers written up. This is the best basis for separation I ever had the pleasure to uncover."

Zhi Lan stifled a laugh. Her gaze strayed to Shao Qing again. He was still with his father across the room, but he met her eyes, looking as if he wanted to speak.

"Zhi Lan! I came as soon as I heard!" Master Dan rushed into the parlor at an impressive speed for his age, his white robes flying behind him. "Child, you've never given me this much trouble before!"

"I'm sorry, Master Dan," Zhi Lan said meekly.

"Never mind that. What happened? Are you alright?"

Zhi Lan quickly summarized the trial to the best of her ability, though her head was still spinning. "I'm fine," she said finally.

"So this is the master painter who started all this trouble," Magistrate Li said from behind them. "Dan Li Chen, I presume?"

Master Dan bowed low. He had forsaken propriety for her, having not introduced himself to their betters when he entered the room. He was generous with his praise now.

"Thank you, Magistrate Li. If it weren't for your fair and just ruling, my student here would be in terrible trouble. You are truly noble, of position and of character."

Zhi Lan blushed and bowed as well. She was still embarrassed about being caught breaking and entering Magistrate Li's house. And despite what Master Dan said, Magistrate Li hadn't exactly been fair or just. He had bent the rules to suit them. Why, he himself was entangled in the thievery by being a patron of stolen art!

Shao Qing was right about the law. Justice never happened as it should.

Magistrate Li returned the bow, his lips slightly upturned when Zhi Lan stammered her thanks. "You had better stick to your ink and brush, young miss. I do not think you share the same talents as my grandson."

Master Dan sighed when the magistrate went to speak to Lady Bu. "I was afraid I wouldn't be able to face your parents after this, Zhi Lan. It's like ever since we got here there has been nothing but trouble."

"Well...we don't have to stay any longer," Zhi Lan said. "Lady Bu says we can leave tomorrow."

"It's for the best," Master Dan said with a shake of his head. "What do you say we go north? I hear there are butterfly migrations through the forest. You can practice painting them."

Zhi Lan smiled weakly. "I'd like that."

Lady Bu ordered more refreshments to be brought to them as Master Dan and Zhi Lan planned their route northward, discussing the inns along the road and the money they had left to spend. Zhi Lan was growing more optimistic as

Master Dan described the paintings he wanted to try his hand at and the new techniques he would show her once they came across worthy subject matter.

Eventually, Magistrate Li took his leave. When Lady Bu stood and announced her desire to rest, Zhi Lan realized the parlor was empty.

Shao Qing was gone. And she hadn't even said goodbye.

THE FOLLOWING WEEKS WENT BY in a blur.

Shao Qing was tucked into a carriage with Magistrate Li, Lady Bu, and the man who was his father. When they arrived at Magistrate Li's manor—through the front gates this time—a woman ran out and embraced him, weeping. The servants called him "Young Master Li" and dressed him in fine silk robes. He was given a room and enough food to fill his belly ten times over. He took baths weekly in clean, hot water.

When the bewilderment had worn off, it was as if he had taken a knife to his chest and everything he had suppressed rose to the surface like an unforgiving tide. For days he thought of Su Su and cried himself to sleep.

They hadn't been blood-related after all. Yet she was just as dear to him.

He recalled one night when they had lain on a bed of dry grass, their stomachs tight with hunger, gazing at the stars through a canopy of overgrown bamboo. Su Su had been fussy and restless, still at the age where she needed to be entertained.

Half-asleep, Shao Qing had pointed to the night sky and drew invisible lines with his finger, connecting made-up constellations.

"That is the great hero, Mu Chen. He rides on an eight foot tall horse and saves all the starving children from the streets," Shao Qing said. "One day he'll come for us and take us to his giant mansion."

Su Su gasped. "An eight foot tall horse? How will we ever get on?"

"Mu Chen has very long arms," Shao Qing said haphazardly. "He won't even have to dismount to grab us."

"I wonder what the mansion will be like," Su Su said, her large eyes glimmering. "Do you think we'll have a feast every day? And a great big peach tree to climb and pick from?"

"I think it'll have whatever you like." Su Su sighed dreamily. "I can't wait."

Shao Qing mussed her hair and told her to go to sleep. She had curled herself against him, her breathing soft and even as she dreamed about great heroes with inordinately long arms. Shao Qing spent the rest of the night wide awake, anxiety roiling in his gut, wondering if they would make enough coin to eat tomorrow.

Now it seemed that his made up hero Mu Chen had taken the form of Magistrate Li and his father. Shao Qing had been swept into a giant mansion that had everything he could ever want. Yet he could not share any of it with Su Su, who had believed the story with all her heart.

It was a cruel joke.

Some days Shao Qing fell back into numbness. It was a different sort than what he had been used to. This numbness was bitter and persistent, like a dull ache from an old wound, muffled yet acute. It hurt to inhale. It hurt to pretend everything was fine when it hadn't been for so long.

His parents threw him worried glances. His mother visited him daily, wishing to get to know him even when Shao Qing barely knew himself.

He did learn more about her, though. She liked wisteria flowers, hated embroidery, and preferred her bird's nest soup atrociously sweet. His father Wen Jun, true to his name, was studious and handsome. He was soft-spoken and liked to watch birds in the garden, often referring to a book with illustrations of different bird species.

The sparrow on the first page reminded Shao Qing of Zhi Lan.

It seemed the only times he wasn't numb or in pain, it was when he was thinking about her. During the days he would replay the conversations they had, smile at the things she had said to him and cringe at some of the things he had said to her. Some nights he grew unbearably warm, his body stiff with wanting, until he coaxed himself to climax with the memory of their kiss. He'd fall asleep, dazed and flushed. Shao Qing had thought pleasures of the flesh were not to his taste, but this was different from the night of false intimacy with the faceless courtesan. He knew Zhi Lan. He knew how kind and passionate and generous she was—he knew her soul.

And he missed her.

Two months passed. When Shao Qing was well enough to leave his room, his father began teaching him how to read. Whether he was horrified that his son barely recognized ten characters in all, he didn't show it. Instead he demonstrated the proper way to hold a brush and the six basic strokes that constituted a character. He read him classic books, folktales, and poems. There was an eager earnestness to Wen Jun. He treated Shao Qing gently, as if he were still the infant boy who had been spirited away. Shao Qing did not inherit his father's love of study, but he applied himself nonetheless, practicing his writing and listening attentively when Wen Jun read. He found that he did not want to let his father down.

When Shao Qing had learned enough characters, he composed a letter to the newly appointed magistrate of Zhu City, requesting him to look into the city's orphanages. He was sure they had not ceased their exploitative practices since he had left. Shao Qing felt more at peace when the letter was received, knowing that for now, he had done what little he could for the neglected orphans.

Some weeks after the summer solstice, Shao Qing and his father sat beneath the pavilion that overlooked the pond, in the middle of one of their lessons.

"Are you happy here, son?" Wen Jun asked.

Shao Qing was copying a sheet of characters. He paused his brush, a drop of ink splashing over his work. He had made his brush too wet again. "I'm content, Father," he said.

"I know you left a life behind," Wen Jun said. "It is not our...it is not my intention to isolate you."

Shao Qing had only left the manor once since he arrived. A servant had gone with him all the way to the bamboo forest in Zhu City, laden with incense and a basket of perfectly ripened peaches. Shao Qing had knelt in a clearing and made a mound of dirt and fallen bamboo leaves, withdrawing a small wooden spirit tablet he had carved himself and sticking it into the grave. He arranged the peaches before it, then burned the incense, its fragrant smoke curling and dissipating in the air.

Three times he kowtowed, his forehead touching the earth where he and Su Su had lain under the stars all those years ago. His tears wet the ground—as potent an offering as wine.

Shao Qing had been selfish in his grief. But now, he vowed to provide for her in the afterlife, something he'd failed to do when they were both living, and hoped that her soul would be at peace.

When he returned, Shao Qing felt that he could breathe again. He never ventured out since. After all, where was there to go? There was food and clothing and shelter inside.

"It wasn't much of a life," Shao Qing told his father. He thought back to his days on the streets, then his days with Yao's gang. He'd spent most of it in squalor, numb to almost everything. The heists were the only high points he could remember. Sometimes he missed Yao and the others for their banter, but he didn't mind his newfound peace.

With his soul back, the quiet life at the Li manor was more interesting than anything Shao Qing had ever experienced. He had forgotten there was a whole spectrum of colors to see. He felt the wind acutely on his skin. There were notes of earth and forest in the air. And the willow trees seemed to sing when a breeze blew by, its boughs swaying like the hem of a silk skirt. He wondered if this was how Zhi Lan saw the world in her artist's rapture.

"That painter girl. Do you think of her?" Wen Jun said.

Shao Qing shifted uncomfortably. Where his thoughts strayed regarding Zhi Lan was not exactly something he wanted to share with his father.

"You are allowed to have visitors, son. As long as they're the respectable sort."

Shao Qing nodded once and returned to his writing. If there was one thing he missed about being a thief, it was his freedom. Respectability had been far from his thoughts—a bothersome thing for the nobility. He found that he chafed under such considerations now.

After a moment of silence, Wen Jun finally said, "I've taken the liberty of inviting her and her master."

Shao Qing looked up at this. "Father, I—"

"They will be arriving today. Very shortly, if I'm not mistaken." A slight smile turned up the corners of his mouth, making him look several years younger. "I have a previous commitment. I trust you'll handle things."

Shortly? How short was shortly?

Wen Jun stood and left before his son could begin to ask, disappearing into the main wing.

Shao Qing stood and paced the pavilion. He considered changing his robe. It was a dove gray, drab compared to some of the other things in his wardrobe. His sleeves were marked with a few ink stains.

He sat again, feeling foolish. Zhi Lan had seen him unwashed in black rags. This hardly signified.

But he knew better now. And he realized he wanted to look his best for her.

Shao Qing made it to the edge of the pavilion before he stopped. His breath caught. Across the courtyard was a girl in white.

She was being led to the pavilion by a servant. Her shoulders were hunched slightly, and she was throwing glances at the wall the two of them had climbed over all those months ago. Shao Qing felt a grin split his face.

Zhi Lan reached the end of the garden path that led into the pavilion. The servant bowed and left her. Her gaze fell uncertainly on him, and she bowed formally.

"Excuse me, young master, have you seen...?" Her inquiry trailed off when she straightened. Her lovely eyes widened. "Shao Qing?"

He tucked his hands beneath his sleeves, not quite sure what to do with them. She looked radiant, her cheeks and lips flushed pink. Her hair was done up in silver pins instead of wood, and she wore a chiffon outer robe, which fluttered in the breeze like transparent wisps of mist.

"Zhi Lan. It's good to see you."

He took an involuntary step toward her, as if his impetuous soul had jumped out before him and was tugging his body along.

Zhi Lan took a step back. "Funny being back here," she said with a nervous laugh.

Shao Qing wondered if he had frightened her in his eagerness. She was a sight for sore eyes. He couldn't believe it had been over two months since he had seen her last, kneeling on the cold floor of Magistrate Bu's *yamen*.

Belatedly, he realized he was being rude. "Where is your master?" he asked. "I was told he was invited as well."

"Master Dan? He didn't come. He's in the middle of a painting and didn't want to be disturbed."

Shao Qing secretly celebrated this. "Do you want a tour?" he said eagerly. He suddenly wanted to show her everything, from the orange koi fish in the pond to the sturdy bristles of his new toothbrush.

Zhi Lan gave him a hesitant smile. "I'd like that."

He led her on a leisurely walk across the courtyard gardens, through the kitchen, along the east wing's veranda, and finally toward the main house where his own rooms lay.

When they had passed through on their heist, Shao Qing's suite resembled little more than a haunted storage closet. Now, the old crib was gone and hangings decorated the white walls. Magistrate Li thought Shao Qing had a taste for dragon paintings, so he frequently gifted him scrolls depicting the creatures. The shelves were now full of books. Wen Jun had lent Shao Qing a few volumes from his collection. And along the latticed walls, the windows were propped open, letting in fresh air and sunlight.

"It's like a completely different place!" Zhi Lan turned in a slow circle, her gaze marveling.

She wandered to his alcove bed and ran her fingertips over the soft bedspread. The absentminded gesture made Shao Qing grow warm.

"Do you sleep well?" she asked.

There was a concerned undertone to her words, and he knew she wasn't only speaking about the comfort of the mattress.

"I do," he said quietly. "I think...I am as well as I can be."

Zhi Lan smiled. "I'm glad."

20

ZHI LAN HAD TO ADMIT that the handsome, smiling young man was completely unlike the thief she had known. His enthusiasm was almost childlike as he showed her his family manor, pointing out the smallest of details, from the wood beams on the ceiling to a crescent shaped scratch on a post.

Wealth suited Shao Qing immensely. He was dressed in fine robes with the wide sleeves of the nobility, half his hair smoothed into a neat top knot and the lower half cascading down his back like a brushstroke. His elegant features were no longer at odds with his dress.

Shao Qing led Zhi Lan back outside. They sat on a stone bench below a willow tree, the breeze rustling the boughs.

Zhi Lan brushed off a few leaves that landed on her, not knowing what to say.

She had donned her best clothes—made of silk, recently acquired. She'd even used a hint of rouge on her lips. Zhi Lan told herself it was because she didn't want to look out of place amongst the lavish manor, but a part of her knew that wasn't entirely the case.

She had thought about Shao Qing for the past couple of months—perhaps more than she should have. She missed having someone to argue with during the peaceful weeks of painting and traveling with Master Dan. Nearly every day she regretted that she hadn't said a proper goodbye. She had assumed if they had a chance to speak again, the right words would find her.

How utterly wrong she was.

"You look well," Shao Qing said. His words, though somewhat stilted, broke the awkward silence. He seemed to have a hard time meeting her eyes, though she couldn't imagine why. Their manners had been so easy before.

"So do you," Zhi Lan murmured. She glanced around the large manor. "Have you adjusted to life here?"

"Somewhat. It takes...getting used to." Shao Qing lifted his arms, looking at his large sleeves like they were extra appendages.

Zhi Lan laughed.

His eyes lit up, a slight smile turning up the corners of his mouth.

"Your parents and Magistrate Li have been kind to you, yes?"

"They have. More than I deserve."

"Everyone deserves kindness," Zhi Lan said. Then, added quickly, "Including stinky vagabonds like you."

Shao Qing chuckled. She marveled at the way it transformed him. It was the first time she had seen him laugh, and it made him twice as handsome.

Zhi Lan suddenly felt shy.

The last time they had been this close, he'd been kissing her senseless. She banished the thought immediately. He probably didn't even remember, being half delirious at the time. Meanwhile, the memory had burned itself into her brain. It had cost her a few restless nights.

"Master Dan and I found another patron," Zhi Lan continued, feeling a blush rise to her cheeks. This she could talk about without embarrassment. After Magistrate Bu had been demoted, there had been quite a buzz about the scholar painter caught in the middle of the whirlwind drama. She told Shao Qing about the marquess who had taken a liking to Master Dan's work, and how he had purchased a few of his paintings and rewarded each of them generously. "Even me, though I've done little else but grind ink," Zhi Lan said with a laugh. "I daresay I have a modest dowry now."

Shao Qing tilted his head at this.

She cleared her throat. "Not that I plan on marrying any time soon. The marquess wants to take Master Dan and I to the capital city next week."

"Next week. That's soon."

"It is." Zhi Lan had barely wrapped her head around it herself. She was happy for Master Dan, of course. She didn't want to admit it to him, but she had grown rather weary of big cities, and missed the early days when they had taken excursions to mountains and rivers. She even missed her village and her rambunctious brothers.

"Zhi Lan?"

She jumped, realizing that Shao Qing had said something.

"Sorry, I wasn't listening," she said sheepishly.

"I said you don't seem excited about the prospect."

"You can read minds now that you've got your soul back, hm?"

He raised an eyebrow. "You wear your heart on your sleeve. It's not difficult to know what you're feeling."

Zhi Lan looked away, oddly thrilled with the idea that he knew her feelings and kicking herself for it. He was a magistrate's grandson, and far above her station. Now he was even more unsuitable for her than when he had been a lowly thief.

"How long have you been learning from Master Dan?" Shao Qing asked.

"Almost a full year now." Nearly one year since Zhi Lan had gone home. She wanted to return with the monetary rewards the marquess had given her, but what then? A part of her was disappointed in herself. She had expected to be further along her career at this point.

"Have you thought about finding your own patron?"

Zhi Lan fidgeted with her sleeves. "No. I'm not sure if that path appeals to me anymore."

After the whole debacle with Magistrate Bu, she realized the drama and fickleness of bureaucrats were not to her taste. Nor was the prospect of being someone's trophy artist, painting only what her patron wanted her to paint. Zhi Lan wanted to be an artist for herself. She figured she was better off selling in the street markets than pandering to one person in particular. Perhaps she'd finally muster up the courage to find a fan maker to mount her miniature paintings. If the common folk found joy in her artwork, that would be enough for her.

Zhi Lan had yet to convey this to Master Dan, but she felt that she would have to very soon.

"What if I become your patron?" Shao Qing said, breaking her train of thought.

Zhi Lan stared at him incredulously. "You? But you don't even like art!"

Shao Qing grinned. "That was before I had a soul. Maybe now I have a ravenous taste for it."

"I doubt it," she said with a scoff.

"I'll follow you anywhere you want to go," he continued, echoing his sentiment from all those months ago. When he had first said it, Zhi Lan figured he hadn't meant it. But now, with his eyes so dark and soulful, she couldn't help but think he was earnest.

"I think I will go back to my village. It's between two mountains. Very remote."

"That sounds nice."

"I'd like to paint rivers and mountains, like Master Dan. I'll need someone to grind ink for me."

"I'll be happy to."

"I'll make you carry all our bags."

Shao Qing nodded. "I'm strong enough for it."

Zhi Lan threw him an exasperated look. Surely he was teasing her.

"You seem to have objections," Shao Qing said. "I know I was rough and rude and offended you countless times. But I can change, if that's what you want."

Zhi Lan wondered at this comment. What could he possibly mean by it? "Don't be ridiculous. I like you as you are."

A hesitant smile spread across his face. "You like me?"

She turned away before she smiled back. "Why do you insist on leaving here? Don't you want to enjoy your new life for a bit?"

From the corner of her vision, his smile faded. "I'm grateful for it, of course. But I'm afraid it doesn't suit me. I...don't feel like myself."

Zhi Lan supposed Shao Qing was used to doing as he pleased and traveling from one place to the next. He must have missed his freedom. But surely he didn't prefer the life of a thief over what he had now.

Shao Qing's throat bobbed. "What I mean to say is, there are rules and expectations here I'm not used to. You're the only one from...*before* that I can meet."

"I see," Zhi Lan said. Perhaps he wanted a respectable excuse to travel and see his fellow thieves. She folded her hands and thought it over. The arrangement would not be an unpleasant one. "I suppose you could come with me. It would be beneficial."

Shao Qing looked up hesitantly. "Beneficial?"

"You're wealthy now. And you're willing to support my painting," she conceded. "It's a practical decision."

He frowned, looking almost offended. "I suppose it is."

She raised a teasing eyebrow. "You know, a thief once told me the practical way for a woman to get what she wants is to marry into wealth."

Shao Qing leaned back into the tree trunk, gazing at her. His face was serious when he said, "I won't be opposed to marriage."

Zhi Lan felt hot. The conversation had veered further than she had expected. "I-I didn't mean to suggest that. Don't tease me."

He covered her hand with his, lacing their fingers together in an intimate gesture. Zhi Lan stopped breathing.

"One of the interesting things about having a soul," Shao Qing said softly, "is that it tells me exactly what it wants. And mine wants yours. Alarmingly."

Zhi Lan looked up at him, speechless. Had he been putting on romantic airs all this time? Her heart pounded at the thought. A memory resurfaced. The dragon had first come to her after being released from its scroll. She originally thought that it was fickle and playful, but *this*?

As much as she and Shao Qing had been through, they'd known each other for less than a week. That version of him no longer existed. Did he truly want her now, or were his feelings skewed by the sudden return of his soul? Perhaps he still wasn't thinking straight.

Zhi Lan began to withdraw her hand. "Are you certain?"

Shao Qing recaptured it. "Souls cannot lie."

She swallowed. It was ridiculously flattering and her heart was beating fast from pure, nonsensical joy. Still, she didn't want Shao Qing to choose her if he didn't truly mean it. She wouldn't want to impose on him, and she respected herself too much to allow herself to be deluded.

"I confess I'm not sure who you are anymore," Zhi Lan finally said.

The young man before her was nothing like the thief she had known. She wasn't sure how to consolidate the two.

"Stay and I can show you." Shao Qing leaned close. Zhi Lan's breath caught when she saw the depth of feeling in his eyes. Carefully, he lifted her chin. She knew what was to come next.

His lips met hers. She leaned into him, seemingly on instinct, unable to hold back a sigh when he deepened the kiss. It was more restrained than their first, but she felt this more acutely. When Shao Qing withdrew, his eyes were full of promises that made Zhi Lan blush.

She raised a hand to her mouth. She would let him kiss the rouge off her lips. Because curse him, she had painted it on for his sake.

"Scoundrel," Zhi Lan said without heat.

Shao Qing smiled.

He was certainly in better spirits now. Zhi Lan realized she wanted to know this lighter version of him. Even if the version she'd known had been tortured, contrary, and soulless, Zhi Lan knew that at his core, Shao Qing was truthful and honorable. He had stuck by her when he didn't have to. He was capable of compassion, with and without his soul.

When Zhi Lan had stepped through the gates, she expected this to be their last meeting. After this confession, however, she no longer had the heart to leave him—perhaps she never did.

"Who has ever heard of a magistrate's grandson marrying a farmer's daughter? I'll be your concubine at best and I'd rather avoid that title," Zhi Lan finally said. It was her one last objection, though a weak one at that. He already had her.

"I don't think my father objects. And...I prefer you as my wife."

Zhi Lan's heart stuttered. She had vowed once to never marry a man for money's sake, and yet here was a man with money asking to marry her, and she was not unwilling to be with him.

Had her principles changed? No. Only her circumstances.

A smile tugged at the corners of her lips. "I won't tell you no. But I would like to go home and paint first."

"Whatever you wish for, wife."

Zhi Lan pushed his shoulder. "Don't be so forward." But she couldn't help but plant another kiss on his lips.

EPILOGUE

ONCE UPON A TIME, THERE was a boy who was afraid.

It was a perfectly fine thing to be, because he had a girl to protect him. In her steady companionship he found safety, and in his she found the same. Some days he wished his sister were there to experience such happiness with him, but she lived on in his heart, and though a part of him knew it may never be enough, he found comfort in her memory nonetheless.

The demon had not yet awoken from its hundred-year sleep, but the loss of the dragon soul would be a minor inconvenience. It had hundreds of years left to live and acquiring another victim would be of no consequence.

The boy and the girl traveled through their great bamboo city. The girl parted with her master, thanking him for all he had taught her. The boy visited his thief lord and his wife, then the proprietor of an herbalist shop who had once been kind to him.

The two passed through many great mountains and rivers. The girl painted them all. When they returned to the village of the girl's birth, her family was overjoyed to see her and likewise welcomed her handsome companion with open arms.

When the boy felt compelled to return to his family, the girl followed him back, because he had followed her.

It was there, surrounded by bustling streets and swaying bamboo stalks, they married and lived happily for many years.

AUTHOR'S NOTE

I don't think I've ever had this much fun writing a book before. The process was surprisingly healing, too, as it provided an opportunity to romanticize parts of my ethnic identity, whereas when I was younger, I could only see and experience the negatives of it.

Early in my writing journey, I've had many qualms about writing Chinese-inspired fiction. Mainly, I never felt qualified to do so as someone in the Chinese diaspora.

What can I say? The diaspora kids really have the worst imposter syndrome when it comes to their own cultures. We are more influenced by the country we grew up in than the country of our ethnic origin. I begin to realize that culture and ethnicity are rather personal things, and there is no one right way to represent them. In general, I think it's important to consider an author's ethos while reading their works, even fiction, as it will provide a clearer understanding of what they choose to portray and how they portray it. So, do keep in mind that I am one Chinese-American gal, and that this story is a representation of how I alone interpret parts of my ethnic culture with plenty of creative license from the American side of me.

To Sway A Soul is set in a fictionalized ancient China with a dash of magic, spun in a fairytale-esque way. It's loosely inspired by the story behind the idiom, *hua long dian jing,* or "paint the dragon, dot the eyes", which involves a dragon painting coming to life when its eyes are dotted. The idiom means to put the finishing touches on something, bringing it to perfection.

This book isn't meant to be historically accurate, so I did blend some historical details here. Zhi Lan wears a Song Dynasty outfit in the illustrations. The first illustration shows Zhi Lan and Master Dan kneeling on low stools instead of sitting on chairs, though I have no idea why I chose to do that since I actually did include chairs in the text itself. The floor sitting, by the way, is pre-Tang Dynasty. I based Magistrate Bu's erotic screen painting, *Scenery at the Spring Palace,* off of a Ming Dynasty painting. This genre of erotic art in ancient China was called *chun gong tu* or "spring palace paintings". (Yeah, they were freaky back then.) Willow trees were symbols of spring and rebirth, which takes on a slightly more sensual tone in erotic art. I thought it would be funny to put Zhi Lan and Shao Qing around a bunch of willow trees as a way of saying, "Now kiss!"

Like Master Dan says, everything we paint has symbolism. Haha.

Speaking of painting, I tried my hand at Chinese brush painting for the illustrations in this book, which has been a very fun experiment. I felt rather jaded about art while I worked on this, so I loved writing Zhi Lan and Master Dan, both of whom have passionate and romantic notions about art, even as they have anxieties of their own.

As someone who went through art school's industry conditioning, being a corporate concept artist, and now attempting to become a freelancer, I wonder if art could be commodified to such a degree without compromising the heart of it or my love for it. Being an artist for a living is a delicate balance between holding your art close to your heart and holding it at arm's length so you don't get hurt, pretending at times that it means less than it does until that becomes true. It is a bargain to the demon that is capitalism—your soul in exchange for money.

This story is dedicated to the creatives who have made their art their profession. It's rough out here! I hope you can find some time to create just for yourself, free from pressure, and preferably without a pervy magistrate threatening to hang you if you don't meet your deadlines.

ACKNOWLEDGEMENTS

This book wouldn't be possible without my editor, Savanna, for being my hype woman and editor rolled into one, and my beta readers, Elsa, Phia, Bekah, Cassandra, Jenni, Allis, Faith, Penny, and Yasmin for giving invaluable feedback. Thanks too, to my sister Liana for being a beta reader and number one supporter!

Thanks to my formatter, Greg, who knocked it out of the park as always. And to Jupiter, who did an incredible job on the dust jacket design for the hardcover edition of this book.

I'd like to express my appreciation for the influx of East-Asian-inspired fantasy books in western publishing recently, because without them, I wouldn't have had the courage to write this one.

I'd also like to thank the other authors in this standalone romantasy novella series, *Tempting Thieves*! Remember to check out the rest of the books in this collaboration for more short and fun standalone reads.

And finally thank *you* for reading this book! I sincerely hope you enjoyed it. It would mean a lot if you could rate and review wherever you can.

www.ingramcontent.com/pod-product-compliance
Lightning Source LLC
Chambersburg PA
CBHW031037310726

48969CB00007B/2014